The Onyx Demon

B.J. Irons

Spectrum Books

Contents

I hope something happens. I'm restless as the devil and have a horror of falling in love and growing domestic.

-*F. Scott Fitzgerald, This Side of Paradise*

Chapter 1

Ace

(Age 16)

You should take advantage of being a Bettencourt. Anyone would kill to have that name. Why not make the most of it and do whatever the hell you want? If I had a nickel for every time I heard someone tell me this or something along those lines, I would be able to pay my own tuition here at Amplestone Academy. And believe me, the cost to go to this secondary prep school for even one year is more than the yearly mortgage on some of the luxury condos on the Upper East Side of Manhattan.

Only the most privileged of children from the wealthiest families across the country have the opportunity to attend Amplestone. The only prerequisite to be admitted was that your family net worth had to be over fifty million dollars. If you weren't recognized by Forbes, then you could kiss your chances at getting into Amplestone goodbye. But the school does hold a prestigious reputation for getting every student into an Ivy League school. I'm not sure if that's because of its academic accolades or because of the money spent to get into here. I highly suspect the latter.

Luckily, I had my own boarding room to myself. All the other boys at Amplestone were required to have a roommate, but my father pulled a few strings and, likely, a hefty check for them to make an exception for me, which I was completely grateful for. My persona was that of a lone wolf. It wasn't difficult for me to make friends, but I just never had a strong motivation to be social or to get involved in sports or have sleepovers and try to sneak some of your parents' alcohol without it going noticed, as most other boys my age did.

However, my adopted brother, Leo, who was two years older than me, was the complete polar opposite. Boys and girls flocked to him. He had that magnetism and charm about him that made everyone drawn in. They wanted to be a part of his world as a Bettencourt, and Leo was never afraid to garner the attention and work a crowd. My brother was never one for just a small circle and tight-knit group of friends. No. It wasn't enough for him to be a big fish in a little pond. He wanted to be the blue whale in the vast ocean.

But I could understand why that was the case for Leo. Growing up, he was never a Bettencourt and, from what I gathered, he slept on the streets with his biological mother, who was a junkie. My father, Magnus, stumbled upon her as he got out of his limo one evening years ago. The woman tugged on the fabric of his coat to get his attention as he approached the door to an exclusive nightclub. She held the hand of her malnourished seven-year-old son as she begged him for cash and cocaine.

Instead of giving her exactly what she wanted, my father had an alternative proposition for the desperate woman. It was bad enough that my father was a ruthless businessman and CEO, but to strike up negotiations with a drug addict living on the streets? Magnus Bettencourt knew no bounds. The city was his company playground, and the man loved making a deal. It was practically an art form to him. The world was his blank canvas, and he was its Picasso. And just like Picasso, Magnus Bettencourt turned people ugly and deformed. He was known to get his way and stomped on the faces of all those around him, not caring who he ruined along the way.

As for Leo's biological mother, she too was a victim of my father's obsession with casting everyone to play Meryl Streep in *Sophie's Choice*.

"*I tell you what, my dear. I'll give you ten-thousand dollars in cash, but on one condition. You give up the boy to me.*" He knew exactly the end result of this entire situation. The woman's psychological dependence and withdrawal would triumph in the end. She handed off her child to the megalomaniac, rationalizing that she was doing her moral due diligence in giving her child a better life by handing him off to this tyrannical stranger, one she could never possibly offer it. And so, the junkie disappeared into the foggy night, a small ant in the colossal city that was New York, never to be seen or heard from again.

Ever since that night, no one in our family has ever spoken of Leo's former mother. He was immediately thrown into our family, welcomed with open arms, even by my mother, Vira Bettencourt. He was distant at first, but then came around to the rest of us in a matter of weeks. Such is the malleable mind of a naïve adolescent.

Leo and I became inseparable, being only two years apart in age. He took on the protective big brother role fairly well up until our teenage years. Then his mind became more preoccupied with other things besides me. Popularity, friends, money, girls. All the things hormonal teenage boys crave permanently remained in the forefront of his mind. They took the passenger side of his Rolls-Royce while I became indefinitely stuck in the backseat.

Needless to say, our relationship became strained, until there was one instance that I was sure would bring us closer together. All it takes is one family tragedy and loss to make you rethink life and reevaluate your priorities. My dear loving mother was rushed to the hospital when I was thirteen. She had fainted in the shower one morning. The loud thud of her crashing down onto the polished honey onyx tiles made our housekeepers panic and rush into her bathroom to find the source of the ruckus. Carmina, one of our longest staffed employees at Bettencourt Manor, let out a shriek that would even put the Sirens to shame.

Everyone paused what they were doing and found their way to standing in the hall just outside my parent's bedroom, watching as my mother was carried away once an ambulance was called. Our limo followed in pursuit of the white box on wheels that flashed blaring red lights in circular patterns with my mother inside. It was my first time ever seeing a paramedic vehicle in person and for some reason I could not help but think of Christmas. The flaring red lights instantly made me think of a certain red-nosed reindeer, or even a bright glittery bow wrapped around a pristine pearl box. Was I being morbid for thinking such things? I honestly didn't know.

But ever since that horrid night, I inherited a habitual pattern that became practically innate to me. Whenever I was in a dire or unfortunate situation, I found myself trying to think of the most pleasant of thoughts. Maybe it was a defense or coping mechanism I used to shudder at the pain and anguish I was taught never to show. And so, I carried this custom with me from then on out, refusing to let anyone ever see me in a sad or angered state. I was a chipper kid who was well mature beyond his years. Perhaps it was my pride at stake or maybe even me declining to play into a fear of being viewed as weak and vulnerable, but I learned to always grin and bear the suffering.

After countless tests, biopsies, and referrals from general practitioners to eventually oncologists, our family received the terrible news that my mother was diagnosed with stage IV ovarian cancer. It was then that I felt the motivation to research all that the doctors had spoken of in layman's terms to explain to my family the physiological nature of my mother's body. *T.N.M.* It was a pneumonic only those who have had cancer, and those who were closely affiliated with a loved one who suffered from it would know all too well. Our lives would never be the same again. And it was only three months later that my mother passed away. The loving matriarch that held this dysfunctional family together was no longer with us. That knot that held the Bettencourts in place would soon unravel, making the love we shared loose and limber. But nevertheless, the Bettencourts were still a firm solid rope at the end of the day. Although we would all grow to shun emotional ties with one another, we would all still share a protective bond that would hold us together for the rest of our lives. Such is the nature of the Bettencourt family name. If you were of the bloodline or shared the last name, then you automatically earned the insurmountable amount of loyalty that that very name brought with it.

I sprinted to my room as the day was coming to an end. Once my final class of the afternoon, Pre-Calculus, had finished, I avoided the small-talk that carried on in the halls. I avoided the mad rush into the cafeteria for dinner. Instead, I purposely isolated myself from the rest of the world. And that meant I remained in my room until 6:45pm. By then, all the boys were done dinner and frolicking around the campus, playing games outside, locked in their rooms drawn to MRPG video games, studying and doing homework or pre-gaming to prepare for a wild party or boozefest.

As for me, there was no better time than to make my way down to the cafeteria to grab dinner. I could make quick work of grabbing my meal to-go and speed-walk my way back to my dormitory to remain unseen and unheard.

While I sat criss-cross applesauce on my black Turkish cotton comforter, I held Gabriel, a worn out stuffed lion, in my lap. It was a toy my mother gave me when I was just an infant. Lions were her absolute favorite animal. They represented pride, power, and all things that were majestic. It was no surprise that she named my brother Leo when my father brought him home.

As I devoured my hoagie I'd grabbed from the cafeteria, I browsed through an online forum on my laptop. Ever since my mother's passing, I needed an outlet to express my feelings. Of course, I could not speak to anyone about it, nor show any signs of stress or turmoil. So, the next best option I could find was creating an anonymous account on *wecanstandagainstcancer.com*. I've read through countless stories of family members expressing their grief and the obstacles they've faced in having loved ones who are either fighting the good fight or who have tragically passed from it.

These stories have resonated with me. Their words were so powerful, a weapon of their own kind, more so than any forged sword known to mankind. Every syllable felt like a piercing blade, digging deeper and deeper into my flesh until it tugged and pierced at my heart with the heaviest of blows. I held a connection with these men and women, who bravely spewed their stories to an unknown audience of strangers. Yet the comments and feedback they received were nothing but heart-warming and caring. This was a world I wanted to be a part of. One where I would easily want to be seen in. For now, I would just remain *heard*. This forum was where I opened myself up at. It was the therapy I needed, yet I denied the need for in my real life. The experience was cathartic. As I vigorously stroked my fingertips against my keyboard, sharing my current feelings and moods from today, I felt a tear slowly trickling down my cheek as it often did on a daily occurrence, making me feel even the slightest bit closer to my mother.

During my Latin class the following day, one of the office secretaries interrupted the lecture. My eyes lifted from my paper and pencil to the front of the room where Mrs. Davinko, a petite woman with thick-framed glasses and a tight black blouse and skirt, stopped midsentence. Her hair was tightly pulled back into a bun. She leaned over to accept the whisper from the woman. "Mr. Bettencourt," she then called out. All eyes darted over to me with wonder. It was the most attention I've managed to get all year long, yet I made it my mission to avoid such a spotlight since my very first day here at Amplestone Academy.

"Your presence is requested in the counseling office," Mrs. Davinko revealed.

"*Ohhhhhhhh!!!!*" all the students exclaimed, going from a low-pitch sound to a shocked high-pitch biting noise.

"Hush!" Our Latin teacher warned them. "Now back to male nominative and genitive verb rules…"

As everyone returned their gazes back to Mrs. Davinko, I quietly closed my binder and laptop, slowly shoving them into my book bag. I didn't bother to zip it up, in fear that the noise would somehow distract everyone to glancing back in my direction. Ducking my head, I made a beeline for the back door of the classroom and softly closed it behind me as I made my exit.

Why would I be called down to the counseling office so suddenly? That was never a good sign. Immediately, the worst of possible fates struck my mind with a deep impact.

Did Leo get into another fist fight? Was he brutally hurt this time?

Was it my father? Was he in an accident?

Had I been found out? Did the IT guys here at Amplestone somehow gain access to my internet search history and discover my account on *wecanstandagainstcancer.com*? Did they review all of my posts and this was meant to be some sort of psychological intervention?

In any case, I knew this impromptu visit to the counseling office meant something awful. I had a sinking feeling in the pit of my stomach. The remains of my protein bar from breakfast this morning began to slowly rise up the length of my esophagus. It was at that very moment I was second-guessing my immediate walk to the office. I debated on stopping to visit the restroom to upchuck my light morning meal, but knew that this was just a fleeting feeling and would eventually subside once I figured out what the deal was.

As I made my way to the front lobby of Amplestone Academy, I entered the main office doors. My eyes glanced over the white marble desk, where the secretary who came to my Latin class was eyeing me down menacingly. I gulped heavily when my blue eyes met hers. Scratching the back of my blonde hair with nervousness, I approached her. "Ummm. I'm here to see the counselor," I softly uttered to her, wondering if she even made out a single word I had said.

Her wrinkly finger pointed towards the back of the office. "Yes, Mr. Bettencourt. Mr. Preston has been waiting for you. You can head back. His door is open," she informed me.

I nodded. "Thank you." My hands squeezed the straps of my bookbag tightly, the redness in my knuckles becoming almost inflamed by how hard I was gripping on to them. Each step I took toward Mr. Preston's office sent a chilling jolt throughout my body the more I neared his domain. Soon, I found myself within his open doorway, lightly tapping on the side doorframe to gather his attention.

The man abruptly stared up from his computer once he recognized me. He shot out of his chair, approaching my direction. "Ah! Mr. Bettencourt. Thank you for coming on such short notice. I'm sorry to have had to pull you out of class so suddenly. Hopefully, I wasn't interrupting anything too important that you were learning?"

I shook my head as he patted me firmly on the shoulder. Mr. Preston was a colossal man at six-foot four-inches. His muscles tugged and flexed against his tawny brown dress pants and white button-down shirt. It would not surprise me if he was once a former pro-wrestler in his former career. Although his physical being was intimidating, his tone and personality were not. They were completely the exact opposite, with how warm and inviting he was, with his sincere smile and caring nature.

"No. You didn't interrupt much," I responded.

"That's great to hear," Mr. Preston added, before softly shutting the office door from behind to give us privacy as I stepped further into the room. "Please, have a seat," he offered.

"Okay…" I removed my backpack from over my shoulder and placed it on the ground beside me, slumping into the chair directly across from Mr. Preston, who had his hands folded together, each finger interlocked with the other. He leaned over his desk, just staring at me with a blank expression on his face.

I knew this was going to be bad, whatever it was that he had to share. Otherwise, he wouldn't have drastically changed this quickly from a man who was thrilled to see me to one who now had a stone-cold expression on his face.

"Mr. Bettencourt, I'm sure you're wondering why you were called down here?"

I shrugged nonchalantly. "I guess so."

"Well, some of your teachers have expressed some concerns about your well-being," he bluntly stated, getting right to the point of the matter.

"My well-being?" I repeated aloud, not quite understanding where this was coming from.

"Yes. They are worried about you, this being your first year here at Amplestone Academy and all. Whenever they assign you to collaborate or speak with other students in class, they claim you sort of shut down and just keep to yourself, not contributing much. Tell me, Ace, do you have any friends here on campus?"

This was much worse than I had imagined. I did not know my teachers thought this about me. I assumed I was covering my tracks with my lack of socializing fairly well, but apparently, this was not the case at all. They were able to quickly dissect me and bring it to the attention of the lead counselor at Amplestone.

However, I did not want to come clean to Mr. Preston. It would be embarrassing to reveal that I did not make a single friend here at Amplestone in the past several months since I first arrived. The natural thing for me to do was lie, as if on instinct. "Of course, I have friends on campus."

"Like who?" he immediately asked, challenging my response.

I was getting frustrated. I rose from my seat, while retrieving my backpack, losing all of my cool. "I don't understand why I'm even here. I thought I was being called down here because something terrible happened or because there was something going on with my family. I didn't expect to be interrogated like this," I brashly accused him.

"Mr. Bettencourt. Please have a seat. I have no intention of disconcerting you."

After taking a few deep breaths to maintain my composure, I listened to his directions and returned back to sitting down.

"Very good," he stated, once he saw that I was sedentary. "Now, I think what you would benefit from is a mentorship program of sorts."

"A mentorship program?" I raised my brow at him. Just what I needed. Another *thing* added to my plate.

"Precisely. I think it would be in your best interest to be taken under the wing of one of the older boys here at the school, someone who can provide you guidance and bring out the extravert that's buried within you. As a Bettencourt, I know you are capable of greatness, and we would be doing you a disservice here at Amplestone if we did not perform our due diligence in helping raise you to be the man you were destined to be."

This was all too much for me. I didn't need to be anyone's charity case. I had no desire to be paraded around the school by an upperclassman like a sad puppy dog. I would be picked on and bullied in a heartbeat. It would mean that I would gravitate everyone's attention towards me, which I worked so hard to avoid. I wanted to be overlooked. Why did no one understand that?

"I appreciate everyone's concern, but I'll have to pass on the mentorship offer. Thank you, though." I rose from my seat once more and turned my back to Mr. Preston. My hand was tightly grasped on the door handle, ready to open it to sprint the hell out of here and return to class.

But before I could even turn the handle, Mr. Preston spoke once again. "Well, if you don't want to resolve this through what we have to offer, then I could always give your father a phone call to see how he would want the situation handled."

I paused, closing my eyes firmly with agitation, letting what he just said fully sink into me. Instantly, I became more vexed.

Was Mr. Preston threatening me!?

But he knew the exact cards he was currently playing. This was his Hail Mary attempt in order to get me committed to this mentorship idea he was so adamant about. For whatever reason, I'll never know.

However, I was in no position to argue with him. The last thing I wanted was for my dad to catch wind of me being anti-social. He had already warned me that if I caused any sort of trouble or issue for him while at Amplestone, that he would ship me off to a militant boarding school in London without any access to electronic devices or the whole outside world. That I could not afford to let happen.

So, I did the only thing I could in this moment. *Give in.*

I spun around, my obliterating gaze darting at Mr. Preston to show him I would be cooperative, but was pissed about this entire ordeal. "Fine. I'll go along with it. But who is this mentor you had in mind?"

The counselor stroked his stubbly chin with his fingertips, as if deep in thought. "Maxwell Brexley," he replied.

My eyes widened in shock at the mention of the name, as if it were a curse word that would damn anyone to hell who spoke of it.

"What? No way. He would never agree to that. Maxwell seems like he would never be bothered with this kind of thing," I explained.

Mr. Preston shook his head. "I'm afraid you're wrong on that one, Mr. Bettencourt. Maxwell has already offered to serve as a mentor to some of this year's new students in any given capacity. And so he will be yours."

Maxwell Brexley… being a mentor to me!?

I could feel the sweat start to form on my hairline. My heart raced like a volatile prisoner in a cell, needing to escape from my rib cage. My breathing rate became abnormal. I was scared that

I could hyperventilate at any moment, because having Maxwell Brexley serve as my mentor was a fate worse than death. It was then that I began to consider moving to London to attend that brutal military school.

Chapter 2

Maxwell

(Age 18)

The thing about trying to always *do the right thing*. It gets old pretty damn fast. Luckily, I learned that at a fairly young age. And ever since then, I've been wreaking havoc over the world.

Well, at least *my* world and anyone who was involved in it.

When people see a misbehaved child or someone who is a consistent trouble-maker, they are quick to blame the mother and the father. But in my case, this could not be further from the truth. Topper and Victoria Brexley are the epitome of loving and nurturing parents. Despite us being one of the richest families in the country, they took it upon themselves to take a more hands-on approach in raising me. It would have been so easy for them to hire five nannies to watch me around the clock, but they took the more difficult route, even with the disposable income.

Topper and Victoria did nothing but spoil me rotten. I received all the best designer clothes from around the world, the most high-end technological toys, and a rigorous education. My mother would often cuddle me in our lavish theater room as we watched a nightly Disney movie together, while my father would brag about my accomplishments at my various prep schools and how mature and intelligent I was for my age.

Unfortunately for them, things would drastically change in my teenage years. In my adolescence, I was pretty scrawny for my size, which was surprising, considering how well-built my father was. I was often picked on in school, pushed into the dirt at the playground, my pants often shanked whenever I was dangling from the monkey bars. Kids would all point and laugh at me. Yet, I remained helpless. A weak little fucker who hadn't the strength nor the power to stand up to the other boys who towered over me, constantly calling me names and making my life a living hell.

But once I hit puberty, I shot up like beanstalk. My muscles quickly thickened at the age of thirteen. I became the biggest student in all my classes, hovering over the masses. No one then dared to lay a finger on me, in fear that I would pulverize the living shit out of them. And they were absolutely fucking right to think that, because I would have.

During my breaks from prep school, my father often brought me into his office to be his shadow. Having only one other sibling, who was my younger sister, Charlotte, I was the only male heir to the Brexley conglomerate. Naturally, I would inherit the CEO position and the entire family corporation once my father reached a certain age of retirement or passed on from this world. Whichever came sooner.

My times spent at his high-rise New York Office were fairly boring at first. Afterall, I was thirteen. What the hell could I have learned from my time spent there? But little did I know that I would be able to pick up on the daily operations of the place rather quickly. I would also become acquainted with all of my father's subordinates. I developed a knack for being able to read people and their true intentions.

His personal assistant, Kelsey, was an obvious slut. Her skirts were just a certain length too short, wanting to reveal the curves of her thighs. Whenever my father told a joke that was barely even funny, she laughed at it way more enthusiastically than was warranted. Her hand flailed and held his shoulder just a brisk too long than one should. Not to mention she interacted with the men in the office much more differently than the women. Her demeanor was lively and flirtatious around the boys. But around the ladies, her face became stern and her eyes often rolled to the back of her head whenever she was forced to have to make small talk or collaborate on a project with them. Yes, Kelsey had no shame. Even when I would eventually turn sixteen, she would make moves on me and be as blunt as possible with wanting to drag me to a private closet to fuck her. But I knew better than to let that vile social-climber get her way. I wouldn't let her have that satisfaction. The desperate fiend that she was.

Claude was another employee that closely worked alongside my father at Brexley Global, except Claude was revealed to be a devious snake. Turned out he was a mole in the company, who leaked confidential information about Brexley's initiatives and up and coming technological advances to our main competitors. Not to mention he also dealt with insider trading, royally fucking with many of our major accounts and investments. Even to this day, we still have ongoing litigation with the man for all of his illegal activities within the company that are still being uncovered from over the years he worked directly under my father.

But Claude and Kelsey were not the only licentious characters that roamed these halls of Brexley Global. There were many others whose true colors I was able to unveil. And the whole experience left a bitter taste in my mouth through my teenage years. My family worked so hard to build this company. Topper Brexley was a man of many skills and talents, with a kind heart. Yet these despicable people that he pulled up the ladder with him were nothing but greedy and money-hungry sons of bitches. If they had the chance to burn my father for a quick lump of cash, I could almost guarantee that they would do it.

These dirty fucking leeches deserved nothing from my father. They should be lucky that he even gives a breath in their direction or utters a single syllable to them. These foul-mouthed rodents should be groveling at his feet even for the morsels of crumbs he offered them, although he gave them so much more.

It reminded me of those early days when I was being bullied at prep school. Those fucking toolbags were lucky I was incapable of using my money and family power to fuck them over. If they really knew what I was more than capable of in the future, they wouldn't have dared to mess with me then. It was about time I started going on the offense and no longer hold up my shield, dealing with the attacks and blows from people that would inevitably come my way strictly based on my wealth, family, and title. I would beat them to the punch and walk all over their miserable excuses for lives before they would ever even gain the chance to make their mark against me.

My father is too good of a soul. He truly is a one of a kind. These people at his company, and all around him for that matter would grow to regret ever having disdain for him, or allowing the thought of crossing him to even graze their minds. For when I became CEO of Brexley Corporation, they would be shaking in their Minolos and Louboutins. I'd give them something to fear, becoming someone they'd never think to fuck with, knowing I would crush them asunder.

Although Topper Brexley was immensely loyal to his family (both his actual family and those who worked under him), the man could still be cutthroat, especially when it came to his enemies and Brexley Global competitors. Specifically, it was those involved with Bettencourt Corporation who proved to be his biggest adversaries.

"That cocky son of a bitch!" my father pounded his fist into his desk, causing me to jump out of my chair directly across from him. It was my last week home before I would be returning to Amplestone Academy, entering my senior year. "Magnus Bettencourt has no shame! He spent more than eighty million to acquire Qatalyst Enterprises from under us. The company was nowhere near worth the amount he paid. The bastard only did it to sweep it out from under our feet!" my father irately shouted.

The Bettencourts and the Brexleys have been at economic war for years. But what was once a professional rivalry has since become personal over the past several decades. My father despised Magnus Bettencourt. The two almost ended up in a physical brawl at the annual Carts for Hearts charity gala last year.

During the Renaissance Era, it was the Capulets and the Montagues who were at odds. At the time of the Reconstruction

Era, the Hatfields and McCoys had their decades long family feud. And now, in this Modern Age, the Bettencourts and Brexleys were up at bat to claim the historical title.

My whole life, I was practically trained to despise Magnus Bettencourt along with his male spawn, who were close to my age, Leo and Ace Bettencourt. I've never actually met the filthy little devils of the egocentric maniac, but that absence would come to a full end very soon.

"I've been informed that the younger Bettencourt will be attending Amplestone this year, as an incoming freshman," my father told me.

I rolled my eyes, with my arms folded across my chest, slouched down in the chair in his office. "Yeah? And why the hell should I care? I don't associate with fresh fish," I spoke condescendingly.

Topper Brexley stood up, pacing from behind his desk, inching his way towards me. "But you will this year. Don't be a goddamn fool, Max! I need you to keep an eye on Ace Bettencourt. If he is set to be the next heir to the Bettencourt Empire, you better be damn sure I want you on him like a hound-dog. He will become *your* problem in the future." My father poked his index finger sharply into my bulging chest. "Do you understand what I am telling you, son?"

Instantly, I swatted his hand away from me. "Yeah. Yeah. Yeah. Keep your friends close and your enemies closer. That whole fucking spiel. I got it."

The old man's face became more stoic when he realized I was not taking this more seriously as he had hoped for. "I'm warning you, Maxwell. You'd do well to connect with that boy. Allow him to trust you. Make him want to play in your sandbox and then be sure to play in his. It's only going to help you out in the long run. Because when the time is right, you'll be able to crush him and his family like the little maggots that they are." He clenched his fist tightly in the air to give more emphasis to his speech.

Despite my asshole persona that I was determined to not let falter, deep down, I knew it would be unwise to disobey Topper Brexley. The man was practically a genius, a mogul. Everything he touched turned to gold. Every prediction he made came true. For every suggestion he made, only a fucking fool would go against it. And I was no fucking fool. So, I would plan to be strategic in how I would approach the Bettencourt kid when I returned to Amplestone. Growing up, I've always loved a challenge and when it came to anything involving plotting and scheming, you bet your ass I was going to revel in it. I'd have Ace Bettencourt wrapped around my fucking finger in no time.

Months had passed since I returned to Amplestone Academy. The Bettencourt boy was as elusive as fucking Carmen Sandiego. Only he was better at keeping himself hidden because he didn't wear a bright ass red overcoat and hat to draw attention to himself. He blended in with the other students at Amplestone pretty well. Either that, or he may have kept himself locked in his dorm room all day and night. Was there some option of enrolling in online virtual classes that I didn't know about that he was taking? How could someone in a school of no more than three-hundred students remain so furtive?

There were times when I could easily spot him from the opposite side of the campus grounds when we were outside. His golden hair was easy to pinpoint, even in the far-off distance. A beacon for all no matter what time of day it was. He effortlessly stood out among a crowd. But when I sped my way across campus to catch up with him, he was nowhere to be found. Disappeared without a trace, the quick and sneaky little fucker.

Early on in the school year, I expected to find him at one of our dorm parties. He was Ace Bettencourt, after all. Everyone at the academy knew of him and his family long before he even began attending this prep school. The entire student body anticipated his arrival, but little did they know of how much of a hermit he truly was. They assumed, like me, a major trust fund teenager would turn out to be the loud, irresponsible, obnoxious party boy, just as I was. I honestly thought the same thing.

The entire situation left me even more suspicious of Ace. Why was he so secretive? Why did he avoid everyone like the plague? Something wasn't quite right here, and a sense of distrust overcame me and my opinion of my pre-destined family enemy. Only people who keep to themselves and out of the public eye have so much greater to hide. What secrets did Ace have to hide? What aces were literally up his sleeve?

No matter how closed off the Bettencourt brat wanted to remain from the outside world, that was completely unaccept-able. I needed to find a way to get myself involved in his life, to become a part of his world, without being the desperate red-headed mermaid cartoon on the rock with waves splashing against me, obsessed with a complete human stranger. I just needed to find the right angle to insert myself into his existence. But how?

An opportunity would soon present itself to me where I finally obtained the leverage to have someone else do my dirty work for me. On my way back to my dorm room from a late night party, I noticed a single light turned on in one of the main office windows I was passing, except the light was barely able to creep through the closed blinds that eclipsed it.

Perhaps it was the alcohol making me micro-obsessed with it, but I found myself more curious than I probably should have been. Ambling across the wet grass from the overnight dew, I peered through the slight opening on the side of the window that the pearl venetian blinds did not fully cover.

It was an office. A few brown leather chairs and an oak table at the far end of the room. I continued to scan the room and then, once my view landed on the messy desk, my eyes widened with great alarm.

Holy fuck!

There was a huge man, naked. His bulging biceps contracted as he held onto another body that was sprawled across the desk, pounding himself into her. But upon closer examination, I knew exactly who these two people were. It was the head counselor, Mr. Preston and the school's Latin teacher, Mrs. Davinko. Her hair was completely disheveled as his hands ran through it. Her nails trailed his body, leaving red scratch marks all across his chest and shoulders from her wild, feral urges.

I wasn't surprised just because there were two Amplestone adult employees going at it like fucking jack rabbits, which was likely breaking some sort of ethical protocol. Fraternizing and all that bullshit. The real shock value came in knowing that both of these corrupt educators were actually married to other people.

There was something about this affair that sent a jolt through me and made my cock hard. Yes, I was being a voyeur and a complete and utter creeper, but who wouldn't? Mrs. Davinko was hot as shit, but even more so, Mr. Preston looked like a Herculean warrior, with sweat dripping down his flawlessly curved muscles.

Before I could rationalize with what I was about to do, I found myself already pulling out my cell phone and opening up the camera app. Clicking on the circular red button, the recording was already underway. I was a teenage boy, for Christ's sake. What else would I do in this situation? When I saw the video timer going from one minute, to five minutes, to soon ten minutes, my grin stretched even wider across my face, synchronously with Mrs. Davinko stretching into various impressive positions to take Mr. Preston's massive cock. It then began to dawn on me that I had struck pure gold with this find. Now it was just a matter of how I could use this evidence to my advantage.

Chapter 3

Maxwell

(Age 18)

I waited until the following Monday to confront Mr. Preston about his sexual indiscretion with Mrs. Davinko, practically galloping my way to the front office with a diabolical smile plastered on my face. Once I entered, the secretary's eyes popped up from her computer screen to glance at me with a rigid expression on her face.

"Can I help you, sir?" she grimly asked.

I nodded, knocking on the white marble top that separated me from her. "I need to speak with Mr. Preston."

"Is this a scheduled visit? Mr. Preston does not accept walk-in appointments," the old hag groggily stated.

Tell that to the teacher who didn't have a walk-in appointment on the Friday night he was bonking her brains out over his desk, I thought to myself.

"No. It's an impromptu meeting I need to have with him. It's very urgent," I replied.

"I'm sorry, sir, but he is currently with another student. You're just going to have to..."

But I immediately interrupted the ancient, rabid bat. "Listen. Do you not know who I am? I'm Maxwell Brexley. Surely, you've heard of my father, Topper Brexley?"

Of course, I would allude to my father to make shit happen. It was the card I often pulled when things weren't going my way. After all, we were paying Amplestone Academy quite a hefty amount, yearly. More than the normal going tuition rate. If I stepped foot in any room, everyone should be catering to every fucking need I had. I was stunned that there already wasn't a red dot on my portfolio or electronic profile or something in this office, letting this wrinkly antique of a woman know who the fuck she was dealing with.

Instead of instantly caving in to my intimidation, she picked up her phone and clicked on the numbered buttons vigorously. "Hello. Mr. Preston?… Yes. Sorry for the intrusion. Mr. Maxwell Brexley is here to speak to you. He claims it's urgent… Sure. I'll send him right back."

She hung up the phone and lifted her dainty hitch-hiker thumb up, pointing in the direction of the counseling offices. "You may head back, Mr. Brexley," was all she stated, maintaining her focus on her monitor, not even bothering to look me in the eye to further acknowledge my presence.

I would do well to remember this instance and lodge it in the filing cabinet in the back of my brain, where I often kept files of those who have wronged me in the past. Just like an unsolved cold case, I would pull them out in the future and make sure to get my revenge on those people who have ever second-guessed or fucked with me. And this bitch was no exception.

But right now, I had a bigger fish to fry. So, instead of further giving her a piece of my mind, I bypassed her and made my way to Mr. Preston's office. Another student was just walking out, holding the door open, as I made my way in, shutting it behind me with a loud thud.

Mr. Preston stared up at me from behind his desk. A desk that was now completely organized with papers aligned neatly on it with framed pictures of his wife and children serving as a decoration, contrary to the tainted state it was in a few nights ago, with Mrs. Davinko's pussy juices soaking it.

"Ah! Mr. Brexley. And to what do I owe the pleasure?" Mr. Preston leaned back in his chair, folding his thick arms over his protruding chest. "Please, have a seat," he offered.

I shook my head. "I think I'll stand, thank you very much," I enthusiastically declared, eyeing the man up like he was my prey. The gazelle was now still and cornered, right where he needed to be. It was only a matter of time before this cheetah would dive and pounce on it for the kill.

"And there will be no pleasure from what I have to say," I added, as I traced my fingers along the framed photograph of his wife and kids, as they stood smiling from the camera on some plain-looking beach with salty, murky blue water in the background.

Mr. Preston had a perplexed expression written on his face. "Is everything alright? Did something happen to you, Mr. Brexley?"

I shrugged. "Oh. Everything is fine and dandy. Nothing at all happened to me. But I should be the one asking you that very question, Mr. Preston. Is everything alright with you? I mean, it sure looked like everything was fine when I caught you with Mrs. Davinko, pounding your cock into her. Although, based on the expressions on both of your faces, it looked like you were the one enjoying yourself far more than she was."

Mr. Preston's eyes practically bulged out of their sockets once I fed him this information that I was privy to. Quickly, he rose out of his seat and made his way over to the windows that you could peer from into the main office lobby. He drew the blinds shut, likely wanting no one to intrude or hear the uncomfortable conversation that was bound to take place here.

He sharply turned around and glanced at me with bewilderment. "How did you…?"

"It doesn't matter how I know you were bumping uglies with a married teacher," I interceded. "All that matters is knowing I'm aware of it, and I have video evidence of the occurrence." I pulled out my phone and held the screen so that it faced Mr. Preston. He watched it intently, being reminded of the office sex scene he had taken part in, one that could easily pass for one of those cheaply produced amateur boss and secretary office pornos that were often seen across the web.

His hand reached to snatch the phone away from me as he lunged forward at me irately. But my reflexes were quick on the draw, and I retracted the phone and side-stepped away from him. He stumbled forward and abruptly turned back to face me as I held my index finger up, shaking it at him. "I've already made multiple copies of the video. This isn't the only one. So, feel free to have my phone and smash it into a million pieces. It will do you no good."

Mr. Preston let out a heavy grunt, mumbling inaudibles which I assumed were curses under his breath at me.

"Do you really think I'm that fucking stupid to not have back-ups? Just who the hell do you think I am?" I asked, raising my brow at him.

"Does anyone else know about this?" he frantically asked, with a worry behind his voice.

"Not *yet*," I replied, before rounding his desk once more, this time grabbing the image of his wife and kids with great purpose, glossing over it meaningfully. "And no one has to know about this, Mr. Preston. All of this can easily go away and we'll never have to speak about it again, so long as you abide by my rules and conditions."

"Your conditions?" he repeated. "I don't have any money, if that's what you're after."

Fucking idiot!

"I don't want your money, Mr. Preston. Nor do I need it." *I'm a fucking Brexley. Duh! My family's swimming in cash. Like your fucking chump change would do me any good.*

"What I need is for you to speak with Ace Bettencourt," I explained.

"Ace Bettencourt? What do you want with him?"

"Honestly, it's none of your fucking business. You should strictly be concerned with what I have in my possession and knowing I am more than capable of exposing you to your wife, the Dean of Amplestone, and the rest of the world, for that matter. I will ruin your miserable excuse for a life if you don't meet my demands," I informed him.

"Fine!" Mr. Preston reluctantly conceded. "What you do you want me to do regarding Ace Bettencourt?"

"It's simple really," I nonchalantly stated, this time taking a seat in Mr. Preston's chair, leaning back in it and propping my feet up on his desk. It was the major power move I wanted to illustrate to show him who was now in charge here. "Ace is a bit of a loner, extremely anti-social, which I'm surprised was not already brought to your attention, with you being a counselor and all. Anyway, the whole thing is pretty damn alarming.

What I want you to do is call Ace into your office. Tell him that there is concern among his teachers about how much of a recluse he really is. Advise him to take part in a mentorship program, one in which I would serve as his mentor. Tell him something along the lines of how I will be taking him under my wing and showing him the ropes of Amplestone. Get creative with it." I waved my hands in the air, attempting to come up with more rehearsed lines for Mr. Preston to use with Ace.

"And what makes you so sure he would be willing to be a part of this mentorship program with you?" Mr. Preston held a doubtful look on his face.

"If he's not willing, then you need to threaten him!" I practically shouted, annoyed that I was the one coming up with this solution. Mr. Preston was the one that was supposed to feel backed into the corner. This was a survival of the fittest predicament he was in. He needed to get on board with this and use his fucking brain if he didn't want his scandal blasted out for all to see and hear.

"Warn him that you will have no choice but to contact his father to seek his advice on how to handle the situation, if Ace does not take part in this mentorship," I further added.

"That's it?" Mr. Preston asked. "That's all it's going to take to convince him?"

I nodded. "Yes. I know the Bettencourts well. There is no way Ace would want to cause any problems for Magnus Bettencourt. It would tarnish his very name and legacy if his dad were to ever think Ace was anything but perfect."

"Very well. I'll call him into my office first thing tomorrow morning," he stated.

"Better yet, do it this afternoon. Cancel whatever appointment you have going on today. Do what you need to do to make it happen as soon as possible," I instructed.

"Fine! And then I'm done Brexley. No more of these little games."

"Of course. Just get the job done and then you won't have to hear from me ever again," I promised him.

And just like that, I had all of my little fucking ducks in a row. I had spent months trying to hunt down Ace Bettencourt, but to no avail, when all along I should have come up with an ingenious plan such as this to begin with. Why waste time on being the one to try and find the fucking runt when I could easily force him to have to come to me?

Mr. Preston gave me a thumbs up in the hall later that day as we passed one another, heading in opposite directions. So, Ace did wind up taking the bait. Therefore, it was only a matter of time before he would present himself to me. He had no choice but to seek me out in order to fulfill this mentorship obligation he now had on his plate. In the meantime, I would just kick back and relax, no longer having to worry about easing my way into Bettencourt's life.

It would be a late dinner for me this evening, having had to stay later after school hours for all that I missed in Calculus class, since I skipped half the lecture just to bombard Mr. Preston earlier with the terms of my blackmail. So, after I finished making up my missed assignment, I made my way down to the cafeteria towards closing hour. I practically devoured my food in just a few gulps before feeling a tap on my shoulder. I twisted my neck only to see Wilson Greenwell behind me. I stared into his hazel-green eyes maniacally before I scanned the entire cafeteria to make sure no one else was watching the two of us interact.

"What did I tell you about coming up to me in public!?" I reminded him, vexed as ever.

"Chill. No one is around, Max, which is exactly why I came up to you now, of all times."

I held a quizzical brow. "And why is that again?"

Wilson leaned over to whisper in my ear while massaging my shoulder seductively. "Like I said. *No one* is around. We've never done it in the cafeteria bathroom yet." He pulled back, giving me a wink.

Like me, Wilson was an Amplestone closet-case. We wouldn't dare to come out at this point in our lives. What would the other boys at Amplestone think? Hell, what would our families think? Especially mine. I had a lot riding on my career in the future. The last thing I needed was for my father to have second thoughts about me reigning over Brexley Global all on account of my sexuality. He would surely hand the enterprise over to my idiot cousin, Jasper, if he learned I was gay.

Luckily, Wilson Greenwell was in the same boat as me. He, too, had a rich family. They owned Florida's leading real estate agency, also having claimed half of the deals on all estates in the Star Island, Miami market. His sexuality was a secret, too. However, it was last year that he came onto me hardcore. He couldn't help himself. After a few shots of tequila, the liquid courage oozed right out of him. I took him back to my dorm and fucked him like my life depended on it. Ever since then, we've been fuck buddies.

Only recently, we started to ante up the stakes a bit with finding new places in public to have sex. It made our fuck sessions all the more intense with the added thrill of possibly getting caught. But just like me, Greenwell loved a good challenge. And so, this sordid sport we found ourselves playing turned out to resume its gameplay once again this evening.

I watched as Wilson strutted across the cafeteria and bared right into the female restroom once he saw none of the cafeteria workers were looking. His bathroom selection made absolute sense. Amplestone Academy was an all-boys school, after all. Also, all employees had their own faculty lavatories they resorted to utilizing. So, I had no doubt we would be safe in this public female restroom. Who the hell would catch us?

I waited a solid five minutes before making my way to the ladies' room, behind Wilson. I surveyed the cafeteria to make sure no one was looking my way. Just a *check my own ass* precaution I took, not wanting to leave anyone with even the slightest trace of suspicion. As I entered the bathroom, I saw Wilson completely stripped down, his ass pressed backward into one of the sinks, his hands curled, gripping the enamel cast-iron end of it.

"Did you bring a condom and lube?" I questioned.

He nodded toward the adjacent sink, where the small bottle of lube and condom wrapper sat.

A grin crossed my face. "It seems like you've been plotting this all along," I seductively groaned, as I scanned over his sexy body.

"Maybe..." was all he uttered as I stepped towards him, gripping the back of his neck with my hand. I tugged it to the side, so that its full surface was exposed to me, like a vampire claiming its victim. Softly, I began nibbling on it, causing Wilson to shut his eyes and let out the inescapable moans from his lips.

"Fuck, baby," he whimpered, as I picked up my rhythm. Wilson finagled his hands to unbutton my khakis and tugged them down with my underwear in one sweep, exposing my rock-hard erection. His palm wrapped around my shaft, massaging it with each stroke he made.

With his other hand, Wilson grabbed the back of my jet-black hair, squeezing onto it as I lifted him in the air, so that his ass was planted on the edge of the sink, legs dangling off of it. My wet kisses trickled down his torso and onto his belly button before they were in line with his ass. Gripping underneath his quads, I lifted his legs up, revealing to me his smooth ass and puckering hole. It practically begged and pleaded for my tongue to slip in it, and so I obliged, pressing my face into Wilson's ass. He yelped the second he felt my slippery warm mouth attempt to bury itself inside him. I ferociously went in on that perfect bubble butt of his, eating it out like it was the last fucking supper.

And Wilson enjoyed every minute of it. His hands reached for the back of my head, pressing on it, as if wanting my tongue to get deeper and deeper into him. "Fuck, that's amazing!" he squealed, before I came back up for air, regaining my breath.

This time, Wilson scooted himself off the sink and got down on his knees on the bathroom floor. He began jacking my dick off while playing with my balls with his tongue. A spark overcame me as I felt his hot breath against my skin. A spark that jumped from my brain and bolted its way down my spine and to my cock with the million other sparks now presiding there.

Soon enough, Wilson wrapped his entire mouth around the tip of my dick, slightly teasing it at first, before plunging his entire mouth forward so that my shaft was fully immersed in his mouth. His head bobbed up and down on it while I clenched my fist into his hair, wanting to control my thrusts into his mouth. It was I who held the power now, while he serviced me, and I savored every second of it. I allowed myself to get lost in the feeling of Wilson's blowjob, closing my eyes and lifting my head up. The fluorescence of the bright white bathroom ceiling lights tried to penetrate my eyelids. But the light wouldn't be the only thing doing the penetrating in this moment. As soon as Wilson was done sucking me, I was ready to bend him over on the sink and fuck that gelatinous ass of his mercilessly.

As I opened my eyes, I returned my gaze back down to Wilson, who continued to go to town on my thick cock. But something else caught my attention, suddenly. I glanced up at the entrance of the bathroom, noticing a figure peeking around the wall. I was half-tempted to stop Wilson and yell at the perv watching us, but I couldn't, because I recognized that person instantly. That golden mop of hair on his head was unmistakable. It was Ace Bettencourt, of all people.

Despite how caught off-guard I was by this whole experience, I continued to let Wilson slurp down on my cock, as I studied Ace carefully. A demonic smirk crept on my face as he continued to watch the sex scene before him. Our eyes met one another for probably longer than they should have, before he spun around and darted right out of the bathroom.

The sound of the door shutting caused Wilson to jump up in alarm. Panicked, he began reaching for his clothes, desperately trying to cover himself up.

"Who the fuck was that?" he whispered.

"No one important," I replied with a grin still stamped on my face. "Absolutely no one important."

Chapter 4

Ace

(Age 16)

I dashed out of the cafeteria like a madman. I felt trapped, claustrophobic in this building until I opened the door and emerged out into the campus courtyard, gasping for air. It was as if I had just come up from a deep-sea dive, finally able to revitalize myself on the fresh oxygen in the atmosphere.

I panted and stopped, but only for a brief moment to catch my breath, before continuing to run in the direction of the dorms. I glanced over my shoulder every now and then, hoping Maxwell Brexley wasn't on my tail, hunting me down like a feral hyena.

It wasn't until I sprinted into my building and up the side stairs, not even bothering to risk the wait time of the elevator, before I came out into the fourth-floor hall. Running up to my door, I reached for my keys in my pocket. Frantically, my hands trembled in fear, as I sorted through my various keys to find the right one that would open this God forsaken door and lead me to salvation. Once I found it, I jammed it into the keyhole and pressed on my door, practically stumbling into my suite. I slammed the door shut behind me, not only locking it but also dead bolting it as a further precaution.

My hands covered my face in terror as I pressed my back into the door, sliding down it slowly, until I met the ground, with my back still against it. I banged my head on it a few times, annoyed by my actions and what I had just done.

Of all the scenes I could have witnessed and of all the people I could have watched, it just had to be Maxwell Brexley. The very exact Maxwell who was the son of my father's greatest enemy. He despised the Brexleys with every nerve in his body. The Brexleys have caused our family so many problems over the years, nearly taking Bettencourt Corporation down. Luckily, my father was able to circumvent their seedy actions and continue to grow Bettencourt Corporation to one of the most successful conglomerates that it is today.

So many questions circled my mind with all that had just transpired.

Why was Max in the cafeteria so late in the evening?

Well, I obviously knew the answer to that. He thought it would be cleared out so he could have sex with Wilson Greenwell in the bathroom. Max probably had no idea another student would even be in the cafeteria that late in the evening, during the closing hour. But how could he have known that that was the ideal time I would grab dinner, to avoid everyone else?

Why did my bladder have to kick in at the worst possible time?

Usually, I would hold it until I got my meal and returned to my dorm. But this time, the urge to pee came on me in a fury. And so, I decided to quickly use the men's cafeteria bathroom. Unfortunately, when I rounded the corner to enter it, there was a yellow *wet floor* caution sign blocking the door, preventing me from entering it. So, with minimal options (and pissing my pants not being one of them), I decided to use the women's restroom and make swift work of it. I would be in and out of there in a flash. No one would even know.

But as I opened the door, I could hear moans and groans sounding like it was coming from two men in there. Without even realizing what I was doing, I softly shut the door behind me and peered my way around the wall, to see the source of the pleasurable noises. My jaw dropped to the floor when I saw Maxwell standing with his pants down, wrapped around his ankles, while Wilson Greenwell was sucking him off. It was then that my need to pee completely subsided, with a new sensation and stimulation rushing to my groin as I watched Maxwell's body jolt with delight as Wilson's mouth engulfed his entire erection. He was stunning, captivating, a descendant of Greek or Roman God. I could not keep my eyes off of him. What had overcome me? Why was I this incapacitated at the very sight of Maxwell almost naked?

Still, part of me knew I should sneak out of here before he would open his eyes and be aware of my presence. Yet, something latched on to me and forced me to remain in place. It was as if an invisible ghost stepped on my feet and held me still, *wanting* Maxwell Brexley to catch me watching him fuck Wilson's mouth.

And that ghost's motive would triumph, for Max opened his eyes and instantly caught sight of me peeking out behind the wall. At first, I thought he would immediately yell and scream when he caught wind of me creeping on them. But much to my amazement, he didn't. He wasn't even fazed by my existence. Instead, he held his gaze on me so confidently, so menacingly, as if he thought I wished it were me on my knees pleasuring him.

Did I wish it were me there, in place of Wilson?

I wasn't even sure. Part of me did. But at the same time, did that make me gay? I never found another boy or girl to ever be attractive in my eyes. Yet, at the very second I saw Maxwell Brexley standing there in all his power and glory, practically owning another human being who was groveling before him, a wild sense of passion overcame me. I wanted to feel his body against mine and what it would be like to have my lips pressed against his. His lips that his tongue was licking as he stared me down intently while fucking Wilson Greenwell's mouth.

Was Maxwell Brexley gay?

I mean, the writing was on the bathroom wall, literally. He could be bisexual, of course, but I felt myself jumping to conclusions, assuming he was, in fact, gay. And now, I was in on his secret. But what scared me the most was *him* knowing that I had this information; that at any moment I could reveal his deep, dark secret to the world and ruin him and his family. And that made me petrified, because I had heard rumors about how ruthless and cruel Maxwell could be. And so, I naturally wondered, would he hurt me, or hell, even try to kill me to keep his secret hidden from the world? I couldn't see why not. He would be more than capable of murdering me and making it look like an accident. The Brexleys had all the money in the world to cover up my death and could easily have me vanish with no form of evidence, tracing my disappearance back to them.

My thoughts were immediately disrupted by a loud banging coming from the other end of my door. The knocks were so intense that they made the door shake, causing my head to bounce off of it.

Holy shit! He's here! Maxwell really is going to kill me!

Soon the noise subsided as I rose to my feet and peered through the peephole, but no one was there. I waited a moment to see if the person who knocked would resurface, but they didn't. I felt possessed. A desperate need to see who it was brainwashed me. I knew who it was, yet I had to see it for myself, with my very own eyes, that it was *him*.

I unlocked the door and removed the deadbolt, before softly opening it. I was literally one of those idiots in the scary movies that I often screamed at, shouting at them to *not go out there*. Then once they made the stupid mistake, I always said, *well, they deserve to die*. Yet here I was, doing the exact same thing I had shouted countless times against doing. Did I deserve to die for being so dumb? Probably.

I popped my head out into the hallway, scanning down its corridors left and right. But there was nothing. No one was in sight. No sign of life.

Letting out a heavy sigh, I stepped back into my room, assuming that the person had just left and would try to return again later. As my hand held the doorknob to push it shut, an instant pressure counteracted me. The door flew open before I could close it. I floundered backwards from the sudden impact and glanced up to see Maxwell standing in my doorway. He stepped forward, slamming the door shut behind him.

Instantly, I ran from the hallway and towards my bedroom, attempting to lock myself in the room, but Max was too quick for me. He was hot on my trail and held his hand up against my bedroom door, preventing me from even closing it. I was now trapped with nowhere to go.

"Please, I didn't mean to…" I began pleading.

But Max charged at me, pushing me hard against the wall with his hand spread, grappling my throat with it. He squeezed tightly. His dark, sinister eyes locked in on mine. I couldn't face him. So, I closed my eyes, refusing to stare directly at him, just hoping my death would be painless and I would wake up in heaven or some other bizarre dimension.

"Open your eyes!" Maxwell demanded. "Open your fucking eyes, now!" I felt his spit trickle against my lips and cheeks as he gave me the orders. I could feel his warm breath strike my skin. He was that close to me.

Having no other choice but to give in, I opened them, revealing my baby blue eyes to him. His fingers curled, tightening his grip around my neck. I gagged, slightly choking from the strength he applied against it.

"You will *never* tell anyone what you saw in the bathroom tonight. Is that understood?"

All I could do was nod, but that didn't cut it for Maxwell. He slammed my head back again into the wall.

"Say it!" he seethed. "Say that you won't tell a soul!"

"I... won't... tell... anyone..." I managed to get out in between able breaths.

His hand loosened up around my throat, but he still held me firmly in place. As I studied his eyes carefully, I knew he was thinking. I could practically see the cogs in his head spinning as I gazed behind those glorious, yet villainous eyes of his.

"But how can I trust you? How do I know you won't run and tell your precious little daddy about everything that went down tonight, including this?" he asked.

Of course he didn't know if he could trust me. He would never know. Maxwell would be putting trust in a complete stranger. A complete stranger that was a part of the family that he despised. Yet, I had to somehow let him know that I meant what I said. I was not like my father Magnus, nor was I like Topper Brexley and even Maxwell himself. I kept my word when it came to promises. I didn't possess a single lying or deceitful bone in my body.

Before I could even think of how to respond to this broken boy, all I could do was pity him. Pity him for holding this deep kept secret from the rest of the world. For being born into this very same lifestyle that I was born into. Both of us being pre-destined to rule over our family companies, never to have any say in what our future looked like. It had already been pre-selected the minute we came forth into this very world. All the pressures, the burdens, the expectations he carried on his shoulders. I held those very same ones. I understood all that he had gone through and may be the only one who truly could possibly empathize with him.

Maxwell's passion was there. I could see it in his eyes. He was a special boy. That very passion of his brought out my very own. A passion that stirred within me, one I never knew existed. All it needed was the proper ingredient to sprout and blossom to life. And Maxwell was that ingredient.

I've never felt anything like this. I had a yearning to feel him. Admittedly, despite the death grip he held on me, the mere touch of his skin against mine sent a rush through me. My mind was no longer acting of its own accord. I was rendered victim to this boy. He controlled my inner workings. Maxwell was at the helm, steering my emotions and cravings through the turbulent seas, and I raised no fight against it.

I relinquished myself to him. And before I knew what I was doing, my neck was craning, counteracting his strength to come even closer to him. My lips locked with his as we kissed. My eyes closed to savor his taste. I was expecting the moment to end abruptly with him pulling away, making my very first kiss a fleeting memory. But I was shocked that this was not the case. Our mouths remained intact, and I even felt Max's hand that was on my throat reach around to the back of my neck, pulling me further into him, deepening our embrace. I was half-tempted to trace my hands up his back to rub him, but feared any other movement from me would trigger him to end this. And that was not an option at this point. I needed his touch, his warmth, more than I cared to admit. Maxwell was my drug of choice, my dependency, and I had no desire to go through withdrawal.

After another minute, he was finally the one to step back, breaking the spell we were under. He wiped his mouth with his forearm, and before I even had a moment to react, he returned to wrapping his hand around my throat, pinning me to the wall, but this time with a wicked grin on his face. "You are so mine, Bettencourt. You don't even fucking know what you just gotten yourself into." Finally, he released me once and for all, moving to the opposite side of the room. I placed my hands over my neck, in the same exact place his hand was at, slowly tracing over the heated area with my fingertips, slowly, soothingly.

As I glance up at him, I could see he was surveying my room, looking around as if searching for something. Reaching down to my bed, he grabbed my stuffed lion, Gabriel, by the head and brought it toward his face, closely inspecting it.

"A stuffed animal? Really?" He placed his other hand over his face, chuckling through it, much to my embarrassment.

Before I could even respond to him, he was already leaving the bedroom with Gabriel in his hand. I chased after him into the main foyer of the suite. "Give it back!" I demanded. "It's special to me."

"Nope. I think I'll take it as collateral," Maxwell replied. "I need to teach you a lesson, Bettencourt, a lifelong lesson, so that you know to never fuck with me for as long as we both live."

He bolted out of my dorm and down the hall towards the stairwell. I called out to him, begging to return Gabriel to me, but he wasn't listening. Maxwell had no clue that the lion was the closest thing I had to my mother. Otherwise, he would have never done something so sadistic as this, in taking it away from me.

But then, horrible thoughts crossed my mind. What if he did in fact know that Gabriel was a gift from my dead mother? What if he was this twisted and demented to want to purposefully hurt me to the core?

I hated Maxwell Brexley! I hated him so much for doing this! The sick son of a bitch!

Yet, I just shared my very first kiss with him. And I could not deny that there was something so irresistible about the boy. He caused a balmy stir within me. I felt hot and lighter in his presence. My cock hardened at the mere sight of him.

I knew this wouldn't be my last time seeing Maxwell Brexley, not by a long shot. In fact, I had a hunch our relationship and journey with one another was only beginning. However, whether the journey would be pleasant or abhorrent, I wasn't sure of, but I suspected the latter.

Whether or not he intended to, Maxwell did things to me that I've never experienced in my entire life. He drew out feelings from within me that even I couldn't explain.

Feelings of torture. Feelings of love. Feelings of disdain, sorrow, and pity. However, there was one thing that I was certain of for sure. I was going to get hurt by Maxwell Brexley. I was going to get hurt so badly by him. And no matter what I did, there was nothing that could ever prepare me for the pain and turmoil I would allow him to inflict upon me.

Chapter 5

Maxwell

(Age 18)

Now that I finally made it out of there, I strode back to my dorm room with the dirty stuffed animal clenched in my fist.

What the fuck was that? Like seriously. What the actual fuck?

It was the first time anyone had caught me in the act of fooling around with another guy. Of all people to have been the one to witness it, it just so happened to be Ace Bettencourt, the one person who has every motive in their blood to bring me and my family down. How could I have been so damn reckless?

But all was not lost. I needed for Ace to realize just who he was fucking messing with, if he thought even for a moment that he wanted to divulge the details of my sexuality to anyone. He needed to be scared, shivering in his bed into the late hours with nightmares about me. I wanted to consume his mind, his fears, his biggest insecurities. That was my sole mission.

This plan was now set in motion. And it started with me accosting the Bettencourt boy in his own dorm room. Everything was going swimmingly until that very moment no one saw coming. *He kissed me.* Ace Bettencourt made the first move in leaning towards me to place his lips against my own. And the worst part about it was that I allowed it. I accepted his soft touch and even acted on it. It was the one time in our encounter that I lost control. A lapse in judgment on my part. A moment of weakness. I gave Ace that power, and now I was regretting every second of it.

The question that I still could not wrap my brain around was why Ace did it? I was a monster to him. A conniving villain. Instead of despising me and wanting to have me killed, he felt the need to kiss me, of all things. Perhaps I should have realized that Ace was gay, too. Obviously, he wouldn't have done what he did if he wasn't. Was this his way of sharing his own looming secret with me, too? Nevertheless, I could not let my guard down around him.

I stroked my fingertips across my lips. Ace's touch still lingered there. The feeling had yet to subside, which was odd, because that was never the case with Wilson. With Wilson, we just fucked and messed around to get our rocks off. But this kiss with Ace... it was something completely different. Something so different that it crept beneath my skin and ate at me. I couldn't understand it, the sort of passion he elicited from me in that minute I remained vulnerable as we sealed the deal.

Maybe it was the shock of the entire situation that left me confused and not acting like my normal self. Getting caught with another guy, meeting Ace Bettencourt for the very first time, while also kissing him. It was all so much in just a short span of time. So much to digest that I still had yet to process and fully think it all through.

Another thing that stood out to me was Ace's demeanor, now that I thought about it. Intimidating him proved to be a fucking cakewalk. I knew the boy was closed off and preferred to remain isolated from everyone else, but I half-expected him to at least put up some sort of fight against me. He was a Bettencourt, after all. Aggression ebbed and flowed in his blood. Enmity coursed through his veins. Yet, this was not the Ace I had encountered. This boy with his back against the wall was a victim. Submissive to a fault. He would rapidly succumb to a more powerful force in the blink of an eye. A force like me.

There were so many things not adding up about him. How could the son of the ruthless Magnus Bettencourt be so timid? So demure. And this was the biological Bettencourt boy we were talking about, not the adopted one. There were no excuses for him.

Or what if this was all an act? What if Ace was putting on a show for me? Maybe he was pretending this entire time, playing some genius psychological warfare game with me, trying to make me think he was this innocent, bashful damsel so that I would never be on my toes around him. Was this his game plan all along, to make me out to be a fool so that he could show his true colors and squash me like a bug when the time came for him to be able to ruin me when I least expected it?

But it was hard to picture that a sixteen-year-old could be such a qualified actor and be able to pull a stunt like this. Maybe I was giving him too much credit.

Ugh! Sometimes my mind was my own worst enemy. Over-analyzing every situation. Predicting every step and turn in the future.

I shook my head, trying to dispel all of these crazy thoughts and emotions.

Get your shit together, Brexley! I mumbled to myself. *This is a fucking Bettencourt we are talking about here. Get your head out of your fucking ass and teach the spoiled brat a lesson.*

I realized there was no point in me trying to decipher who the real Ace Bettencourt was. It honestly didn't matter. Big picture: I needed to shake things up and give him a warning so that he knew to never fuck with me. That was the end goal. Screw the nuances in between. My focus should be on how to send a message to Bettencourt, so that it was crystal fucking clear that I was never to be trifled with.

And then it clicked. I held the pathetic stuffed lion up in front of me, scrutinizing it carefully. A plan began concocting in my head. This stupid little children's animal would literally be my ace in the hole to setting the record straight with Ace Bettencourt.

Chapter 6

Ace

(Age 16)

I wish I could say that I was not used to restless nights of sleep, but I would be lying to myself if I did. Ever since my mother died, I tossed and turned, stirring myself awake in bed multiple times throughout the night since she passed away three years ago. I had dreams of being with her. There were also nightmares making me recount those horrible and tragic scenes in the hospital leading up to her death. Usually I woke up, jolting out of my bed panting, my body full of perspiration, soaking my bed from the night sweats that came with the terrors.

Now, a new figure would consume my mind in the middle of the night, besides my mother, except this person was nowhere as loving and doting as she was. This individual was a hateful and volatile behemoth that went by the name of Maxwell Brexley.

I laid in bed, just staring up at the ceiling. The room was dark, except for the small traces of light that crept in through my blinds from the campus lamp posts outside.

Tonight, I didn't even get the chance to wake up periodically every hour or so as I typically did. There was no opportunity to even have a dream or a nightmare because it was physically impossible for me to fall asleep after what went down this evening.

I found out Maxwell Brexley was gay. Hell, I learned even I was gay. I had met him for the first time in the flesh. Actually, I saw *all* of his flesh for that matter and the very thought of it sent a tepid thrill throughout my body. All within the small span of that same evening, he aggressively pinned me to a wall, ready to choke me to death, kissed me, and then stole the closest prized possession I owned, the thing that held the greatest value to me, Gabriel, my lion that my mother had given me. A vessel that brought me all the closer to her, despite my mother no longer being a part of this world. I held emotional ties to that stuffed animal. And now, it was in the hands of the person that hated me more than anyone else in this world.

Today had been one whirlwind of an experience. The most hectic roller coaster ride of my life and yet, at the same time, the shortest one I had ever been on. You would have thought all of the draining chaos would be enough to knock me out cold and put me right to sleep. But nope. The unpredictability of Maxwell Brexley kept my mind racing. Left me jittery as ever.

Not to mention this was the first night in so many years that I've slept without holding on to Gabriel. There was a dependence there I never knew I was that attached to. I felt lonely. I missed my stuffed lion. I missed holding on to him. But most of all… I missed my mother.

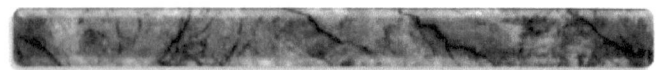

When you wish upon a star, makes no difference who you are…
Anything your heart desires, will come to you…

It was the third time I hit the *snooze* button on my alarm clock on my phone. I had this same alarm song for the past three years since that very fatal day that would change my life forever. It was my mother's favorite Disney song. I often heard her humming it around our home when I was little, over and over again. The instant I heard the lyrics, I always thought of her, and so I decided to make it my morning alarm clock hymn, wanting to wake up every day to memories of her.

It was only an hour or so ago that I had finally fallen asleep. But innately, I knew postponing the inevitable of waking up and getting out of bed would only make me late for my first period class of the day and I could not afford to miss any of my lectures. All it took was one absence to trigger a robo-call and an instant email that would be sent to my father, informing him of my truancy and I did not want to risk that single tardiness as being the death sentence that would send me off to a military boarding school across the Atlantic Ocean.

So, I forced myself to toss the comforter off me and rise out of bed. I checked the clock, realizing I only had thirty minutes to get myself together to get to class on time. I would have to forego a shower until tonight. I darted to the bathroom, brushing my teeth and hair, before applying deodorant. With haste, I put on my clothes and grabbed my bookbag, rushing out of my dorm.

Now that I realized I still had ten minutes left until the first bell rang, I could relax and walk to class without having to make a mad dash across campus. But that was only half correct. I could definitely walk to class, but being *relaxed*… that wasn't in the cards for me today, not after last night's debacle.

As I ambled across the courtyard, I was highly attentive to my surroundings. My eyes were a 360 degrees surveillance camera, searching all around me, petrified that Maxwell would pop out from somewhere and hurt me.

No. That wasn't right.

He was too smart to actually physically assault me in public. He would make some haphazard situation happen that would kill me. And he would make sure it looked like a fluke accident so that he could get away with it. That, I was more than certain of.

Nevertheless, I was on red alert until I safely walked into my first class. And luckily, I made it successfully there without being harmed, giving a deep sigh of relief the second I took my seat at my desk.

Maybe I was overthinking this whole thing. Perhaps Max would just leave me alone altogether and he would only come in contact with me if I ever spilled his secret to the rumor mill. But I knew there was a snowball's chance in hell that that would ever happen. The very same hell that Maxwell Brexley reigned over.

For now, though, I was in the clear, and could focus on my schoolwork. A nice distraction from whatever it was Max likely had in store for me.

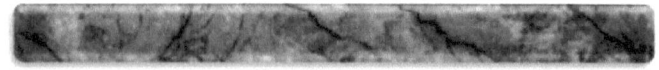

The remainder of the day continued to turn out to be pretty normal, despite my fears. Things proceeded regularly in all of my other classes. No issues. No surprises. No sudden shocks or outbursts. That was until Latin class, of course.

Mrs. Davinko was reviewing some of the prefix and suffix vocabulary terms to help us remember their meanings in Latin.

"And *acetum* means vinegar," she shared with the class. "Is there a term in Anatomy and Physiology class you all learned of that has a similar name?"

A boy named Hector Romero, who was seated in the front of the class was the only one raising his hand. She called on him. "It sounds like *acetabulum*, which is you hip bone socket," he shared enthusiastically with pride in knowing this random fact.

"Exactly! Very good," Mrs. Davinko lauded him. "So, there is actually a morbid historical connection to this. What could vinegar have to do with your hip socket? Well, in ancient Roman times, *acetabulum* referred to a vinegar-cup. Emperors were often fond of vinegar during their meals and typically had a cup full of vinegar on their tables during feasts. And because the hip bone socket looks very similar to the vinegar-cups used by the Romans, it was then anatomically referred to as the *acetabulum*. Also, just to spoil your lunches, it was rumored that in medieval times, people would use hip bone sockets as wine and vinegar cups in their taverns and drink form them," she added.

"Ewwwww!" everyone screeched.

"There's no way that's true. Is it?" Caleb Martin called out.

Mrs. Davinko shrugged. "It's a rumor, but I guess we will never know. Will we?"

She then returned to the board to go over the next vocabulary term, before a loud gasp disrupted the entire class.

All heads turned to the source of the noise. It was Caleb who was up and out of his seat at the window, pointing towards the center of the courtyard. "Look! What the hell is that!?"

"Language!!!" Mrs. Davinko shouted.

"Fine. What the *Infernum* is that!?" Caleb corrected himself in Latin, like the smart-ass that he was.

But no one was paying attention to anything he had to say. They were all now scattered to the far end of the room, trying to push their way towards a front and center view of one of the windows to see what was going on outside.

Mrs. Davinko too rushed over to the window closest to her desk to see what everyone was entranced by. She placed her hand over her mouth once she saw it.

Curious, I too rose from my seat, trying to get a view of what had caused the major distraction. I cut my way through the crowd to get a good view outside. My eyes darted in the direction that everyone's finger pointed in.

The second I saw what the fuss was all about, I had a sinking feeling in the pit of my stomach. A dark cloud was cast in my mind and it rained a gloomy sensation over the rest of my entire body.

Up on the flagpole that was closest to our building was a head. But it wasn't just any head. It was the chopped off head of a stuffed lion, with red residue dripping from its neck that had cotton dangling out. Likely ketchup from the viscosity of it.

I recognized that lion instantly. It was Gabriel. However, no one else around me knew this, nor did they know who it belonged to. The whole scene was enigmatic to them. All the students began whispering to one another, trying to hypothesize the meaning behind it, none of them coming close to being remotely accurate.

Mrs. Davinko picked up her classroom telephone and immediately dialed the main office number, shouting. "Yes. Someone needs to come outside and remove it immediately. What a disgusting thing to do!" she exclaimed.

She was sort of right. It wasn't just disgusting. It was *beyond* disgusting. Cruel, perverse, vicious. Completely inhumane. All I could picture was my mother up there. A second death. Because that was what Gabriel meant to me. It was a second life I had with her, my only connection to the woman I loved. And now she was dead again. Her head hanging from that drawstring, blowing in the breeze.

Instantly I was having an out-of-body experience. I was becoming queasy. I managed to push some of the other students out of the way to get to Mrs. Davinko's desk. "Bathroom?" was all I uttered to her.

She was still distracted by the phone, but she managed to nod to me. "Go ahead, Ace," she replied.

I didn't give it a second thought. I couldn't even bother to fill out the bathroom pass that Mrs. Davinko expected us to sign before we left her room. I barely made it through the hallway and into the bathroom stall before I fell to my knees, practically puking my brains out into the toilet.

I hacked into the bowl for a good five minutes, unable to contain myself. Gabriel was no more. He was turned into a crude statement piece, made by Maxwell Brexley.

What a fucking sick human being!

My vomiting continued. I began to regret any pity or sorrow I felt for him. He definitely was a broken piece of shit. I couldn't believe I even kissed that repulsive shithead. If I had known he was so cruel and capable of this, I would have never been so gentle and meek in his presence. He did not deserve that, not by any means.

How could I have been so stupid? So naïve.

And now Gabriel was no more. He was dismantled... *fucking decapitated, for Christ's sake!*

The only tangible thing that connected me to my mother was no more. Completely gone and beyond repair.

Once I had finished upchucking all of my feelings, I could sense that my cheeks were fully flushed, not because of the after-effects on my sudden sickness, but due to my newfound fury. Never in my life had I felt this burning energy within me, this uncontrollable temper that needed to be unleashed. Although I had no mirror in front of me, I pictured my eyes transitioning from their gentle blueness to a turbulent red hue.

Maxwell Brexley deserved the worst possible fate known to mankind. What kind of person had the audacity to take a kid's stuffed animal his dead mother had given him and make a repugnant mockery of it? It was beyond foul, beyond any vicious adjective, really. There was no way to describe his actions.

Yesterday, I thought Max had brought out a wild, heated passion within me. I was partially accurate with this. Although previously, I thought it was one related to *love*. But now, this passion he had drawn out of me was one of *hate*. I despised Maxwell Brexley, all of the Brexleys for that matter, realizing that my father was right about *their kind* all along. They had no souls. They were reincarnated versions of the devil himself.

Maxwell Brexley had awakened a sinister being within me, one that even I had no control over. And I was determined to bring the bastard down, and his entire family, for that matter. Max had unleashed a wild animal.

It wasn't enough for him to just fuck with me. Now, he brought my mother into it. My family. And blood is thicker than water. He had unchained a Bettencourt beast that he had no idea existed. This irate beast would make him pay for his actions. I would make him regret this sick message he sent my way for the rest of his life until the very day his miserable corpse rotted in the ground beneath me.

Chapter 7

Maxwell

(Age 18)

It was just a fucking stuffed animal. What's the big deal? I thought to myself.

I could have done far worse to Ace Bettencourt. And I have actually done a lot worse to many others before him who have tried to fuck with me. If anything, Ace got off pretty easy with merely a decapitated lion flying from the flagpole.

Nevertheless, it would send a clear message to him. And the intent was for him to realize that I could do horrible things to him and go unscathed during the aftermath. Yes, there were surveillance cameras all over campus. Yes, we had plenty of security guards on patrol that roamed the grounds of Amplestone Academy often. Yet, I would go undetected and not get into trouble for my crude actions. That was one of the perks of being a Brexley, a Brexley who had so much dirt on people it would take a whole year just for Page Six to blast out all of the fucking intel I'd gathered on idiots over time. The Amplestone security officers were no exception.

So, my charade of messing with Ace Bettencourt went off without a hitch. Everyone on campus by now was talking about it. Pictures were posted all across Instagram and Snapchat. But the best thing about this whole enigmatic debacle was that only

Ace and I knew the true meaning behind the actions and all parties that were involved. He was the only student who knew I hung his pathetic little lion high in the air for all to see. And at the same time, I was the only person who knew that said lion belonged to him, unless he showed the embarrassing fading creature to someone else on campus, which I highly doubted he did. Otherwise, that news would have spread like a wildfire. I could see the captions and headlines now: *Isn't the Bettencourt boy a little too old to be playing with stuffed animals? #weak #pathetic #growthefuckup.*

My father did say to get close to Ace Bettencourt, although he meant for me to befriend him and get in his good graces. However, once Ace found out I was hiding in the closet, all bets were off. I would definitely get a lot closer to Ace, just not on the very exact terms my father had intended for.

But here's the thing with Ace, I had him right where I wanted him. The fact that he kissed me spoke volumes. I awoke something in him, an inner beast that was desperate to be untamed. He wanted me, badly. That much was made clear. I could see the longing fervor in his eyes when my hand was spread across the length of his throat. There was a deep desire to have me. His lips quivered with the need to feel mine. They needed the attention to the point where Ace could no longer contain himself.

His inner cravings were like my very own. And if he had deep-seated feelings for me and a lust that was that uncontrollable, it meant that he too had a dark side, just like every last one of us Brexleys and Bettencourts. A dark side that was calling for me, that would always pull him towards me, despite his better judgment. And it would be that dark side that I would be sure to constantly tap into, because as long as it remained alive and unextinguished, Ace would be submissive to me, allowing his carnal pleasures to give me permission to triumph over any rational thought and feeling he possessed.

The evening after the lion scandal, Wilson came over to my dorm. We waited until late at night before he could come by for our usual rendezvous, which consisted of foreplay, him sucking me off, and then me bending him over and making him my moaning bitch. Quick, routinely, calculated, but a much-needed release.

As I opened my front door to let him out, I popped my head into the hallway to make sure the coast was clear before Wilson would speed-walk his was out of here and back to his own dorm. Now that I had my nuts drained, worn out from all the grinding, I was completely ready to pop open a beer, lounge on the sofa and veg out on some trashy reality television.

But before I could even make it to the refrigerator, a loud disturbing rumble at the front door, followed by a second set of obnoxious knocks disrupted me. "Chill the fuck out! I'm coming!" I shouted.

Whoever the impatient fucker was needed to calm down. Instantly, I thought of Wilson, and became aggravated. He knew better than to draw attention like that, especially in front of my dorm room. And why would he feel the need to come back to my dorm to begin with? Unless he forgot his wallet or phone or something, but I was pretty certain he already grabbed everything he brought with him off from my nightstand.

As I came up to the door, I tilted my head and popped my eye through the peephole, but found no one there.

What the actual fuck!?

I opened the door and turned my head down the right side of the hall, but it was completely empty. As I twisted my neck to the left, I felt a huge amount of pressure pound into my chest. Before I knew it, I was forced to step backwards several steps from the sudden impact of being bombarded. The door slammed behind the person that had apparently just pushed me.

It was Ace, and the look on his face said that he was not one happy fucking camper. Not in the very least. It took every ounce of control in my body not to punch him, but I knew physical violence, especially with a Bettencourt, was against all codes of conduct. My father would rip me a new one if word got out that I had assaulted a Bettencourt. It would turn into a giant media frenzy that would affect some major clients and investors of ours, and that was a big fucking no-no.

"What the hell, Bettencourt!" I yelled, completely caught off-guard by this sudden outburst of his. But something wasn't right with Ace. I could see it in his face. His nostrils practically flared like an angered bull. The hostile glare he sent my way was nearly palpable. This was definitely not the same Ace Bettencourt I encountered last night.

"What do you mean, 'what the hell, Bettencourt?'" He bared his teeth at me. "I should be the one saying that to you. What's your problem, Maxwell? How could you do something so... evil to me?"

I raised my brow, astonished that he had the balls to address me in such a way. It was a rarity that anyone came at me in an aggressive manner and stood their ground. Something that hadn't happened since I was much younger on the school playground, pushed around by kids twice my size. Yet here Ace was, at least a good thirty or so pounds lighter than me and more than a head-length shorter, charging at me like a minotaur.

"Evil!?" I chuckled, laughing in his face. "Attaching a stuffed animal to a flagpole is a far outcry from evil. Honestly, you're lucky that's all I damn well did. You should take your fucking blessings and move on Bettencourt. Let it be a mild warning to never fuck with me."

He shook his head, stepping closer to me. His proximity was a little disturbing, since he was acting unpredictable, leading me to further back away from him towards the wall.

"You fucking moron!" Ace hurled at me.

Fucking? It was the first time I ever heard him curse. Not that the word "fucking" was obscure to me or anything. In my word cloud of most over-used words, it was probably the one that was in the largest size font, dead center, in a bright vibrant color, surrounded by many other smaller, less meaningful words in my lexicon. But hearing Ace say it was different. It left a foul taste in my mouth. There was something about him saying it that left me bitter. And I didn't like it one bit.

Perhaps it corrupted my initial thoughts about him being this docile, innocent deer that he was and, instead, made him seem like a mighty, unwavering stag. But I was the stag. He was the deer. There couldn't be two stags here, especially when it came to our future. If I wanted to move Brexley Global forward with as much momentum as possible when I become CEO then I need to be the more powerful one. I needed to beat Ace Bettencourt at every single corporate game I knew we would be playing in the future. And let's face it, what deer would stand a chance against a sharp antlered stag?

"I'd watch your mouth, Bettencourt. Wouldn't want you to regret what comes out of it," I coolly stated.

He shook his head and stammered his foot, defiant as ever. "No. You don't understand. That lion… Gabriel." Ace paused, as if what he was bound to say next was painful to even share.

So, the raggedy plush toy had a name? And it was beyond anything I wanted to hear. This conversation and the amount of attention I was now forced to give to this fucking stuffed animal irked me to no end.

"Out with it!" I demanded. "What was so important about that stupid fucking lion?"

It was then that I regretted my own comments here. For a second, as I gazed into Ace's eyes, I could have sworn they had a red glint in them. A flame that burned brightly. My words had given life to this Phoenix that was now rising from its ashes. Although this Phoenix was heated with temper, resentment, and determined vengefulness within it.

Before I could even process and react to what was happening, I found myself pinned to my own wall, Ace's hands wrapped around my throat, clenching it tightly.

My, how the tables have turned…

"It was a gift from my mother!" he finally came out with, as if he was finally able to release all this pent-up rage within him. A bottle with so much built pressure that finally exploded with the pop of its cork. Now it just spilled all over without anything blocking its path. "It was the closest thing I had to her since her death. But now… it's ruined! Gone! All because of you!"

I could feel his grip now tighten on my neck like the small vice that it was. Clearly, I hadn't realized how my actions would affect Ace in this way. I mean, who the hell could have predicted this outcome? No one. That's fucking who.

Yet, in this instance, something still clicked in me. Ace was, in fact, hiding in his shell. His whole silent and desolate demeanor was a coverup. Like me, he too carried demons on his shoulders at all times. Only his demons were focused around all the chaotic emotions brought on to him from the death of his mother, Vira Bettencourt.

I had heard about the death of Magnus's wife, Vira, three years ago. The news made national headlines. Only those who lived under a fucking rock didn't know about it. But the Bettencourts remained private when it all happened, refusing to take any interviews or reporter questions about the death of Vira and how it had an impact on their lives. They purposefully avoided the limelight and all flashes and cameras for a good few months before they re-emerged, making their public appearance once again. Only when they did, they seemed chipper as ever. It was as if the dark cloud of Vira Bettencourt's untimely death had ceased to exist. I found the whole thing to be pretty fucking bizarre. But then life went on, and Magnus Bettencourt still was up to his old tricks again, resuming the attempt to make my father's life a living hell.

Despite Magnus Bettencourt being a vindictive, heartless golem, he was still one strong son of a bitch. So, it was no surprise to me when he came back to life in the corporate world, after his wife's death, with guns blazing. Yet I failed to consider how the two sons, Leo and Ace, were affected by all this. By association, I assumed they handled it just the same as their father. They were Bettencourts after all. Yet now I was slowly, but surely, beginning to realize that Ace was the black sheep of the family. Nothing remotely similar to Leo or Magnus.

However, this ruthless side of Ace that I was now facing, it was the first time I finally seen the Bettencourt ferocity elicited from him. And all it took was me destroying the one thing that bonded him to his late mother.

Right now, there was nothing that would make this go away. Ace's hatred for me was apparent and valid. I couldn't blame him. So, I simply uttered the words I knew he needed to hear. Two words that I've never spoken of in my entire life. Not to anyone. Yet here I was bound to Ace, needing to give this to him.

What the fuck was coming over me?

"I'm sorry…" I barely mumbled. Despite his fingers pressed into my throat, I could have made it audible to him, but felt the need to keep it as hushed as possible.

"What did you say?" he asked. His eyes widened, just as equally surprised by my apology as I was.

"I said I'm fucking sorry!" I grunted. Now I was becoming more vexed, but not at Ace, instead, at myself for choosing to be this vulnerable. This defenseless. I didn't give a rat's ass about Ace Bettencourt, yet here I was, giving him exactly all that he needed and wanted.

I scanned over him, trying to gauge his reaction to my one and done apology. It was the only verbal reparation I intended on ever giving for the rest of my life.

So, take it and fucking run with it, Ace Bettencourt!

His expression then changed to one of bewilderment. He seemed confused and unsure of what to do or say next. Was he at a loss for words?

Honestly, I had no idea what to do next. I couldn't even budge. I was rendered still, allowing him to still clench his hand on my neck.

We both stood there in silence for a few seconds, just staring at each other. Our breathing rates escalated from the surging tension between us. His chest was rising and falling deeply, while the exhales through my nostrils were intense.

Ace and I could both sense this tension that existed. We had a fire within us that could not be contained. And like a burning wildfire, the flames needed to spread, to find other adjoining blazes to keep it going. His grip on me loosened as his head moved closer to mine. I could feel it. The next action we would take. It was inevitable. We were too drawn into each other at this point to avoid it.

Our lips collided against each other, igniting that spark that needed to flare. God, it felt so fucking good to taste him again. It was the craving I never knew I needed. And what I would give to strip him down and have my way with him. But I knew pushing it too far would likely trigger him. For now, I would unleash all the angst I had within this passionate kiss.

My hand tugged on his golden locks of hair. Ace's own hands made their way down my throat to caress my thick pec muscles. He squeezed them firmly, but then pushed me away. My head flung back, hitting the wall with a thud.

"No!" he abruptly shouted. Although it was unclear as to if he was addressing me or himself. "I can't do this. *We* can't do this. You're just toying with me. My emotions. My feelings. You want me to feel this way, don't you?"

It was difficult to respond to him. He hit the nail on the head, but I refrained from letting him know that. It would only create more of a problem between the two of us.

My lack of a response only prompted him to continue on with his tirade. "Well, let me tell you something, Max. I hate to break it to you, but you won't be getting your way this time. I don't accept your apology and I don't forgive you. I will *never* forgive you for what you did to me. You can plot all you want and do all you can to try and ruin my life, but here's the thing, I have nothing else left to lose. The Bettencourt title, the fame, the wealth. None of that matters to me. I already lost the most important thing in my life. So, none of your vicious stunts will ever hurt me in the way you think that they will. But you, on the other hand..." Ace's index finger jabbed me in the chest. "The secret I have on you would damage you and your family so badly. You have so much to lose from this. I obviously share the same secret and would go down with you in the process, but it's you who cares far too much about your reputation and your family business than I do with my own."

Ace then back-pedaled away and turned his back from me. He stormed over to the front door and placed his hand on the handle. "You would do well to know that I'm the one that really holds all the cards, Maxwell. Your very fate and future depend on me. I have the knowledge that would ruin you. So go on... live your life and become CEO of Brexley Global. Do what you were destined to do. But know that I can pull out that rug from under you whenever the hell I want to."

He opened the door and stepped into the hall, glancing over his shoulder one last time at me. "Don't ever try to fuck with me again, Brexley." Ace slammed the door behind him, leaving me alone in my dorm room to myself.

I remained still, completely lost in all that had just transpired.

What the fuck just happened!?

I could feel the stress begin to consume me. It gathered in my stomach and then started to slowly travel up my body. All of this completely backfired on me and the worst part about it was that I didn't see it coming. Not even from a mile away.

It was the first time in a very long time that the results weren't as I had predicted. I was strategic, calculated, and swift in my actions in making sure I would come out of them on top, completely unscathed. But this situation with Ace... it was far more complex than I had anticipated it being.

I had underestimated the Bettencourt boy, and that was my mistake. He wasn't this naïve teen who could easily be manipulated by me. I had to give him far more credit than I had initially done. He had the fucking audacity to actually stand up to me and even pose a threat. Fucking balls of steel that one had.

I could not help but smirk in this moment. Despite all the shit that Ace now had on me that could jeopardize my future and stake in Brexley Global, all I could now think about was that boldness of his. That lingering kiss that buried itself in the nerves of my lips to make a permanent home there.

Despite how much Ace loathed me, despised me, hated me, there was a part of him that was enthralled by me. Even he could not deny the chemistry that was there between us. We were two different chemicals that were eager to combust whenever they came in contact with one another. And as fucked up as his mind was about me, I had to admit mine was the same with him.

My hands covered my face while I shook my head in disbelief, realizing all that I did to Ace. I had popped the bubble in his perfect, innocent little world. He was now a product of my own creation. I had turned Ace Bettencourt into this perturbed monster. The very same monster that I was.

Nine Years Later...

Chapter 8

Maxwell

(Age 27)

"Cancel my five o'clock, Marta. Grigory Toshima is in town and wants to discuss Brexley Global's future plans with Toshima Enterprises. Book us for six o'clock at Adour at the St. Regis… no, just the two of us is all." I pressed the off button on my office speaker.

Things had drastically changed in my life this past year. For the last six years, I oversaw the Brexley Global whiskey line among other ventures our family company had major stakes in. But it was just three months ago that my father decided to make the difficult decision to step down as CEO of Brexley Global. He advocated for the Board to support his decision in successfully transferring the power over to me to be the new CEO. It was no surprise that the decision and vote was unanimous, and all Board members backed his wish. I had worked my ass off for this company and made all the right moves and actions needed to prove my worth and propel Brexley Global further into being the mega-conglomerate that it was. All my hard-work and dedication was paying off, and I was finally starting to see the fruits of my labor.

Now that I was in charge, I ordered for a "re-org." It was every executive and director's worst nightmare to hear that word at a company. But I needed to clean house. I needed to surround myself with people I could absolutely trust. And I knew for a fact that some of these bimbos my dad kept on his payroll were either worthless or deceitful, for the most part. Topper Brexley often turned a blind eye to many shady ongoings within the company. But this new Brexley CEO was not having it. I had eyes on the back of my head and I was not going to put up with any of that bullshit. Not on my watch.

A knock at my massive mahogany office doors drew my attention away from some of the analytics I was reviewing. I glanced up from my computer to see an all too familiar face. He rubbed his finely manicured hand through his neatly swayed back brunette hair. An unlit, skinny cigar hung from the corner of his mouth. I could not help but smirk. My pretty boy cousin, Jasper, always tried to dress and appear intimidating to cover-up the fact that no one in their right mind could take him seriously, especially after the stunts he pulled during many of his college frat parties and seedy vacations he took in Ibiza with countless men and women riding him while being recorded. You couldn't find a free-porn site that didn't have a video of Jasper. His conquests were stamped all over PornHub and every site that began with an X. Needless to say, I would forego ever stepping foot into the Balearic Sea knowing all the fucking germs and spunk that boy has added to it.

"And what do I owe the pleasure, cousin?" I asked, leaning back in my chair, folding my arms behind my head.

"I would refrain from using the word *pleasure* so soon. You're not going to like what I have to say," he replied.

Jasper tugged on his carmine-shade suit jacket as he came forward, plopping himself down in the caramel leather seat directly across from me. I've only ever seen him in a suit that was a shade of red: maroon, burgundy, scarlet, vermilion, wine, you name it. It seemed as though he had clung on to the name 'Jasper' literally. Brick red jasper stones were a symbol of comfort, strength, security, and healing, none of which coincided with my cousin's personality. Well, except for *healing*, which was exactly the phase he was going through now, attempting to heal and repair the actions of his past in order to move on in his future.

I had put my neck on the line for my dear cousin, giving him the opportunity of a lifetime that he sure as hell did not deserve. But I had to throw him a bone and give him a chance to make a difference for himself. Give him some motivation and something to be devoted towards, which was why I hired him as my COO just two months ago.

It came as a major shock to our critical investors and stake-holders at Brexley Global when I made the announcement. And Jasper was well aware of the risk and sacrifice I was making by bringing him on board at this high up of an executive level. He knew he had better bring his A game, because any fuck-ups on his end would reflect poorly on me. And there was no way I would allow him to ever make me look bad and get away with it.

But so far, Jasper has proven to be a competent and loyal COO. I must admit, I was thoroughly impressed with his performance thus far and how quickly he could catch on to things. The initiative he has been taking has not gone unnoticed and as a reward, I wanted to start including him in some of the high-stakes meetings with clients I was typically involved in. Show him the ropes a bit.

"And what am I not going to like about it?" I asked, in response to his foreboding greeting.

"Grigory Toshima is in town," he began with.

"Yeah? So? I'm well aware. I've booked a six o'clock dinner with him at Adour. He wants to chat about Toshima Enterprise's future here at Brexley Global," I informed him.

"And by that, you mean a non-existent future, right?"

I sat up in my chair now. This conversation had taken a fucking wrong turn that I was not expecting. Jasper's response left me perplexed. I gave my cousin a quizzical look. "What the hell are you talking about?"

Jasper let out a deep sigh, which immediately let me know that whatever the hell it was he was about to say, he didn't really want to confess it. And I knew I would be fucking pissed the instant he did.

"Toshima Enterprises plans to take their business elsewhere. They want to pay us outright for a contract termination and move on."

What the fuck!?

I slammed my fist down hard against my black onyx desk, with white and gray veins flowing through it. The entire office rumbled from the impact.

"And how the fuck do you know this, and I don't!?" I growled, grinding my teeth with rage.

A sly smirk developed on Jasper's face, once he realized he was finally one step ahead of me in something, which was rarely ever the case. "Let's just say I have my sources. A few tight-knit friends over at Bettencourt Corporation leaked the information to me," he admitted.

None of this was adding up. It made absolutely no fucking sense, and my patience was beyond the point of wearing thin. "And tell me how exactly the Bettencourts know about Toshima's decision before everyone else…"

The second I finished that sentence, everything was becoming clearer. All of the knots in this messy rope were finally unwound. Jasper then confirmed my suspicion. "Because that is where Toshima Enterprises is now going, with Bettencourt Corporation."

Those fucking sneaky Bettencourt bitches!

It wasn't just a mere coincidence that Grigory Toshima wanted to close his deal with Brexley Global out of the blue and then just so happened to be picked up by Bettencourt Corporation. Only a fucking idiot would be dumb enough to believe that uninhibited sequence of events.

No. There was shady work at play here. It didn't take a fucking rocket scientist to know that Magnus Bettencourt likely had some private conversations with Grigory Toshima while his company operated under Brexley Corp. He was attempting to undercut our deal and bring Toshima over to the Bettencourts just like he has tried with many other major accounts and clients over the last several decades. Magnus was a dirty, conniving shrew. Under previous circumstances, my father would have played this game of chess with Magnus from the side, making quiet subtle moves against the Bettencourts to get revenge on them for fucking us over again. But not this Brexley. I wouldn't stand for it. I was never one to sit in the shadows and be a sniper from afar. I confronted my problems head on.

Rising from my seat, I went to collect my jet-black suit from the golden coat hanger in the corner of the room, before placing it on, over top of my Dolce and Gabbana black damask patterned vest and matching tie. "Get your shit together. We're leaving," I commanded to Jasper.

My cousin shot right up, scratching the back of his head with confusion. "And where exactly are we going?"

"To Bettencourt Headquarters. I need you to call and arrange a meeting with Magnus Bettencourt right now. We settle this shit once and for all." I moved to my door to open it, before glancing over my shoulder at Jasper to give him one final instruction. "Oh, and let's make it a family affair. Invite the Bettencourt prodigy too."

"Both boys? Or just one of them?" Jasper pulled out his phone and began typing away on it.

"Just Ace. Not the other one. I can handle only so many fucking Bettencourts in a room at once." Stepping out of the room, I trailed down the corridor towards the elevator, with a devious grin on my face.

It had been so many years since prep school when I last saw Ace Bettencourt in person. And I knew he would never turn down this meeting I had planned with him, his father, and Jasper. It wasn't in his nature to refuse the chance to see me. His curiosity to see how I was doing would succeed in the end. And like they always say, curiosity kills the cat. But in this case, I would be the one killing.

It was time to bring back some old memories. Rehash some of those deep and lingering emotions Ace and I had endured at Amplestone Academy back when we were teenagers. I was completely ready to tackle this head on with the utmost fucking confidence. But the real question that remained a mystery was if Ace was ready to face me again.

Chapter 9

Ace

(Age 25)

Was it my dream to take over the business? No. Not in the slightest. But being the first male son in the Bettencourt family doesn't leave many options. I've faced the pressures of having to experience a rigorous education, go to the top business school in the country as well as being heavily involved in Bettencourt Corporation as much as possible since I left Amplestone Academy.

And I had to come to terms with the reality of my situation and my lifestyle. I'm sure most people would think *poor little rich boy. If only most of us had the problem of being a famously destined wealthy CEO. Sooooo sad!* Maybe I was being a little spoiled and rotten, but I'm allowed to express a disinterest no matter what my economic status was, right? There was no passion there. I felt no flutter in my heart in dealing with Corporate America.

Luckily, I didn't get thrown headfirst into being the CEO of Bettencourt Corporation right away. My father, Magnus, was on the verge of handing over the seat to me. However, once news spread that Topper Brexley was retiring and his son Maxwell would reign as the head of Brexley Global, it lit a new fire under my father's ass. With a fresher prey now at bay, he wanted to use his much greater skills and expertise to hunt it down. Now was his chance to really crush the Brexleys when they were in such a vulnerable state, with their company in the middle of a transition state.

Secretly, I was beyond grateful I still had time to bide before all of this unwanted pressure would come barreling down on top of me once I was forced into the role of Bettencourt's CEO. And at the same time, I was also thrilled my father would be the one who had to handle Maxwell Brexley head on. I had no desire to even associate with the arrogant, egotistical asshole. Ever since the lion incident at Amplestone Academy, I steered clear of Maxwell, never wanting to set sight on him for as long as I lived. Surprisingly, Maxwell never once approached me in the last nine years. I assumed he would attempt to threaten me somehow, since I was still the keeper of the secret about his sexuality. Based on the tabloids and social media blogs, Maxwell was still deemed as one of People Magazine's top sexiest bachelors for the fourth year in a row. Yet, there was no indication or any headline that Maxwell Brexley came out as gay.

But the same couldn't be said for me. Against my father's wishes, I publicly announced my homosexuality during my senior year of college. My father and I went through a three-year rough patch after that. It wasn't until the news stories died down and our major investors and clients didn't seem to care that he finally started coming back around. As an apology token, Magnus made me in charge of Bettencourt's Non-Profit Organizations. Specifically, it was our biggest NPO that I fell in love with. The Positive ViBes Charity Foundation, in honor of my mother Vira Bettencourt, was dedicated to helping fund advanced research in finding a cure for Ovarian Cancer. This was truly the best gift my father could have ever given me.

Forget the silver Lamborghini Sesto Elemento that I can count on one-hand the amount of times I've actually ever driven in, and the villa vacation home in Via Mulo, Capri that overlooks the majestic blue Scoglio Unghia Marina that I've only been to three times, or even the Harry Winston diamond watch he got me. No. I never asked for any of those frivolous things. The fact that I was now running a charitable organization that would make a difference in the world… that was the best thing Magnus ever gave me. It was my greatest passion and what I wanted to live for. It was my mission to grow The Positive ViBes Charity Foundation, and I worked tirelessly supporting the cause, planning events, and raising awareness. Being a philanthropist was much more up my alley than being a businessman.

I just wished my father could respect my desire in wanting to stay put here, instead of grooming me to take over his position. If anything, it was my brother, Leo, who was more adamant and devoted to the Bettencourt conglomerate. He was a much better fit for the role and would suit it well, more than I ever could. Yet, my father was headstrong about having me in charge, likely because I was of his sperm… his blood. Poor Leo always got the short end of the stick, being forever reminded that he was the adopted son of Magnus and Vira Bettencourt., the bastard who would always play second fiddle to Ace Bettencourt.

And for that, Leo would continue to resent my very existence. Our relationship continued to digress over the past several years with so much at stake. I continued to remain in my calm and docile bubble, whereas Leo was always on edge and high-strung over everything. He and I both knew he deserved to be next in line to claim the Bettencourt throne, but because my father thought otherwise, Leo decided to since take that decision out on me. Still, he continued to play the part of the doting son well, despite the cold exterior he put on whenever he was in my presence, like he was doing so now. It was his only option if he wanted to play in the Bettencourt sandbox. Leo had to continue to be nice to my father, despite his disdain for the choice he made in selecting me as the next in line.

The tension that existed whenever the three of us were in the same room was so thick it made a Real Housewives reunion seem harmonious. This very tension lingered in the office now, where Leo and I sat next to each other, across from my father, who called us in to meet with him as a matter of urgency.

It was very rare for Magnus to ever make an unscheduled appointment to see me, his own son. But even so, whenever there was an impromptu summons, I knew it meant that something horrible had happened. I sat firmly in the leather chair, my palms tightly squeezed around its gold studded arms, causing my knuckles to turn a faded scarlet, preparing myself for the brutal impact of whatever it was my father had to reveal to us.

"It seems we have finally provoked the Brexley boy. He requested to meet with us immediately," my father informed us.

My ears instantly perked up. Both Leo and my eyes widened with shock, although mine with an even greater alarm.

"And what the hell does he want?" Leo asked, folding his arms over his chest.

"He wants to meet in-person right away. I received zero context as to why, but I already know what it's in regard to," Magnus replied, with a sly grin on his face.

I shrugged, unsure of what my father was referring to, but Leo seemed to have a clue.

"Likely our acquisition of Toshima Enterprises," my brother answered.

"Precisely," my father laughed out loud. "Maxwell Brexley probably shit his pants the second he heard Grigory Toshima was folding with them and placing his bets with us."

The idea of taking major clients out from under other companies left an awful ulcer in the pit of my stomach. It was something Leo and my father were so used to, yet I didn't want to be a part of anything like it. The deceit, the conniving, the manipulation, all of it was too much for me. And I knew that once I became to CEO of Bettencourt Corporation, it would be an expectation and something I would have to get used to on the regular. Still, the very thought of it made me sick to my core, knowing of all the corruption that still occurred between our family and the Brexleys.

Leo raised his brow to our father. "And will we be meeting with the overrated frat boy?"

"Yes," Magnus replied, tapping his fingertips against his desk almost maniacally. "I have arranged for the four of us to meet in our dining quarters. A private chef is on the way."

This was no surprise to me. It was always how Magnus conducted his meetings, over wine and meals you would practically salivate over. Although, it was questionable whether he was possibly micro-dosing his guests or sneaking substances into their drinks unbeknownst to them. Somehow, he always came out on top at the end of these sorts of meetings with the results of negotiations being skewed in his favor. The man never left a lunch or dinner date without a smile on his face. That was for certain.

Leo rose to his feet. "Great. I'll meet you both over there. I have to run back to my office for a moment."

"Meet us over there?" Magnus gave my brother a perturbed look. "Who says you will be joining us? It will just be Ace and I meeting with Maxwell and Jasper Brexley."

My gaze shifted up to Leo, whose cheeks drastically turned beet red when he realized what my father was insinuating. "But I was the one that single-handedly landed Toshima in our territory. I put in the work. That was all my doing. And you're telling me you're going to let Ace, who has no fucking clue about the Toshima account, sit in on this over me?" His fists clenched tightly and shook with aggravation as he spoke to my father.

Magnus shrugged nonchalantly. "It's out of my control, son. It was Brexley who specifically made the request for just Ace and I to be in attendance. No one else."

The beat of my heart ceased pumping for a moment when my father revealed this aloud. *Maxwell was the one that wanted me present? But why? What was his game here?* I thought to myself. My nerves, which felt as if they had been in hibernation for the past nine years, were now fully activated. A geyser was discharging its steamy water all in my stomach when I realized I would have to be face-to-face with Maxwell Brexley once again.

All of those feelings I once felt years ago were rushing in all at once in a full force maelstrom and I was at the center of this turbulent whirlpool. I honestly had no idea how I would handle myself around Maxwell. I hated him. I lusted after him. I was drawn to him, but at the same time, completely repulsed by his very being. My mind was a clusterfuck of mixed emotions, and it was impossible for me to even pin one of those emotions down.

The sound of Leo storming off and slamming my father's office door shut behind him shook me awake from my daydream. I stood and turned to follow and chase after him, but Magnus held his hand up in protest. "Let him be, son. He will get over it. And you needn't concern yourself with your brother's feelings. The only thing you should be focused on is bringing your 'A game' to this meeting. Who knows what sort of tricks the Brexleys have in store for us. You need to be prepared and on your toes the entire time. Do you understand?"

I bowed my head to my father, heeding his words, carefully. "Yes, father."

"Good. Now run along and don't be late for our little luncheon soon. And when the time comes, I want you watching Maxwell Brexley like a hawk, never taking your eyes off of him when we meet. You need to study your opponent to know him like the back of your hand. After all, in just a few years, he will be *your* problem and no longer mine. You'd do well to remember that."

Little did my father know that I didn't have to remember this. I already knew it. Maxwell Brexley had been a problem for me since I was at Amplestone, and I was fully aware that he would continue to be a nuisance to me for years to come. So long as I was a Bettencourt, and he was a Brexley, we would continue to remain each other's problem for an eternity.

"I promise I won't be late. And I will do my best to..." but I couldn't even finish my sentence. My father had slammed his fist down against his desk, interrupting my reply.

"No!" he shouted, vexed by my response. "*You will do your best,* implies that you are *trying* and I cannot afford for you to merely *try*. You must *succeed*. You're a Bettencourt, for Christ's sake, Ace! Start acting like one, especially if you want to have a future as the next CEO."

All I could do was nod, knowing that no response I could give would please my father. Also, I feared that any word I uttered he would immediately contradict me over and further scold me for.

I had no desire to get into an altercation with my father right now, for he would be my one and true ally going into this luncheon with the Brexleys. I needed to remain loyal to him and stay in his good graces, especially when we would be among our sworn adversaries. Because I could only afford to have one enemy on my plate right now. And that spot was strictly reserved for the onyx demon himself, Maxwell Brexley.

Chapter 10

Ace

(Age 25)

Almost all rich men have the impatience of Joffrey Baratheon. Couple that with being as demanding and bold as Scarlett O'Hara and you have yourself one hell of a fierce creature. Magnus Bettencourt was no exception. When he made an order, he expected results to happen at the speed of light. And when they didn't, that's when you would feel his wrath.

It wasn't difficult for one of his many personal assistants to get a private chef over here. They already had one on standby in case my father would randomly schedule a luncheon or dinner to be held in his office or at one of his compounds, which he often did. Needless to say, the retainer fee that was offered to said chef was so exorbitant it made Wolfgang Puck's salary look like a minimum wage. Magnus could afford the best, and so he got the best.

I've been struggling with my view on this throughout my entire life. Was it something to be admired that my father went after what he wanted and got it right away? Or should I frown upon it, realizing just how impatient of a megalomaniac he was over the years as a result and how vulgar and cruel he could be to some of his staff and employees whenever they weren't quick enough to meet his impossible timely demands?

At any rate, the chef was already present, standing beside the long, opulent mahogany table in our private dining hall the second my father and I walked in.

"Mr. Bettencourt," the man removed his white chef hat, revealing his shiny bald head, as he bowed down. "A pleasure as always, sir."

"Ah, Leon! And what have we on the menu this time?" my father asked, shaking the man's hand firmly.

"Well, we have three options anyone can select from: a Lobster Frittata, A5 Japanese Kobe Beef, and an Earthy Florette Salad for our vegans."

"And the caviar on these plates... what type is it?" Magnus asked.

"Almas... only the rarest for you, sir." Leon replied.

Leon received a heavy pat on the shoulder for this acceptable response. Well, really, it was the only acceptable response the chef could give.

"Very good," my father stated. "Although I'm sure the Brexleys won't take notice of the cost of this luncheon. They wouldn't know class or sophistication if it bent them over and..."

But before my father could even finish his crude remark, our attention was diverted to the dining hall entrance, where two tall, muscular men were being escorted our way by my father's assistants.

One wore a burgundy suit and looked like he was some soap opera actor playing the role of a businessman today, who I presumed to be Jasper Brexley, the newly appointed COO of Brexley Global. And to his right, adorned in all black as always, was the infamous Maxwell Brexley. It wasn't a coincidence that he was absent of every color but black. This was typical Maxwell. In ninety percent of the photos I've seen him in over the years, it was the only color he sported. In a home design blog I came across recently, where he showcased his palatial high-rise penthouse, almost all of his furniture was black too. But what struck me was a quote in the article that was supposedly made by him: "*You'll find that my kitchen countertops and most of the tables in my home are made of onyx. Onyx is a symbol of regeneration, instinct, and intuition. I couldn't think of a more appropriate symbolic stone to incorporate into living arrangements… my life, for that matter. And between you and me, Patrick, it's rumored that onyx has a way of heightening your sexual desires.*"

After reading that article, I could feel my entire body contract with a flowing heat moving throughout it. I envisioned myself sitting on Max's black onyx countertops, with his body pressed into mine as he kissed and ravaged me. Yes, I deeply despised the man, but my attraction to him was something that could never be lost. He was my first kiss and undeniably the sexiest man I've ever kissed in my entire life. I've had my fair share of boyfriends over the years, but none of them compared to Maxwell Brexley. The man exuded confidence, masculinity, and sex the second he walked into a room. And it was exactly what he was doing now, as he narrowed the gap between us.

My arms became limber, legs weakening as he continued to approach me. *Come on, Ace. Get it together!* my conscience was chanting, but it was my inner saboteur who was screaming louder and getting his way. I could already feel my cock begin to harden at the mere sight of him. Maxwell had grown up so quickly. At prep school, he was already much taller and broader than most of the other boys, but who knew he could continue to grow and become this mammoth of a man? My god, he was… well, exactly that. He looked like a sculpted god, created by Michelangelo himself.

For a brief second, his gaze met mine, but it was at that instant that he immediately shifted his focus over to my father, choosing to no longer look me in the eye. I felt it then. Call it a spark or even a passionate moment that shot between us, but I definitely felt it and I know he did, too. It was why he avoided me now, so that he could focus on the business matter at hand.

"Maxwell Brexley. Jasper Brexley. We are honored to have you here at Bettencourt…" My father began to greet the intruders with, except his attempt at a formal introduction was instantly abridged.

"Cut the bullshit, Bettencourt!" Maxwell ruthlessly interrupted. "My dad may have been civil and played this stupid fucking Joan Crawford versus Bette Davis game with you, but I'm not going to pretend to be fake and I don't expect you to be either."

My mouth gaped, practically dropping to the floor. In my entire life, I've never heard another human being speak to Magnus Bettencourt in such a rude way. Honestly, whether I witnessed it or not, I imagined no one ever did talk to him with such crass. That is, until now. And although I should be horrified by how aggressive and bold Maxwell was with my father, I was actually thrilled about it.

The thought of someone taking a stand against the almighty powerful Magnus Bettencourt was wild, and to actually be able to see it happen first-hand was maddening. My eyes scanned over Maxwell in awe, and I had to resist myself from jumping on top of his massive body to fiercely kiss him. He was so magnificent right now. So stunningly flawless.

"Hmph. Very well. Let us take a seat and get right down to it then, shall we?" My father held his arm out wide, signaling for everyone to take their seats.

Of course, one of his personal assistants put place card holders on the table, strategically making sure that my father and I sat directly across from the Brexleys. Not that we even needed the names on the cards to tell everyone where to sit. It was evident as ever that no Bettencourt would be seated next to a Brexley. Not in a million years.

As we sat down, two servers came out. One offered a selection of expensive wines and liquor options, while the other shared the three lunch selections that our private chef, Leon, spoke of earlier to us.

"I'll take a glass of your Willett, on the rocks," Max shared with the waiter.

"I'll have the same," Jasper chimed in with.

"Actually, let's get it around the house for all four of us," my father requested to the server.

Of course, this meant I would have to be forced to drink bourbon, which I absolutely hated. The taste of it was so strong and not my cup of tea. I'd prefer wine over liquor any day of the week. But, if I wanted to sit at the *big boys' table*, I supposed I would have to abide by their rules, even if it meant having to suck it up and drink a glass or two of bourbon. I would just have to do my best to hide the squeamish look on my face from the burn, after swallowing it.

"And you can leave the bottle on the table. Better yet, make it two bottles. Based on Mr. Brexley's stress level that he so brazenly showcased just moments ago, it sounds like he is going to need quite a few drinks," Magnus coolly added. My father may not have been as direct as Maxwell was with his insults, but he managed to get his jabs in so furtively and yet effortlessly at the same time, like a hidden sniper on the side ready to make his point-blank shot.

As we finished placing our food orders, the server quickly returned with our drinks and the two bottles of bourbon before running off to give us our privacy.

"So. Grigory Toshima…" Maxwell trailed off, as if someone else was expected to finish his thought for him.

"Yes. What about him?" my father asked with indifference, holding his cards close to him. He gave Maxwell no reaction to be able to read.

"Don't play coy, Bettencourt. Acting coy is cute and all if you're a virgin schoolgirl, but when you're a wrinkly old prick, it's just plain creepy," Maxwell replied.

It took every ounce of control not to spit out my drink across the table by his shocking remark, but I somehow kept my cool.

"You damn well know you pulled some sneaky shit with taking Toshima Enterprises out from under us. So, what exactly did you offer him, Magnus?" Maxwell raised his brow to my father, who merely shrugged.

"I am not at liberty to say, Mr. Brexley. You know the terms of our contracts are strictly confidential. Business School 101. Surely, you went to business school, no?" If anyone could keep up with Maxwell's quick-witted banter and insults, it was my father. He was just as equally fast on the draws.

Maxwell gave a light chuckle to my father's snide comment, brushing it off as if it was something he couldn't even be bothered with. "I don't care if you fess up to it or not. But let me make this crystal clear for you, Magnus. If you ever try to fuck with me, my company, or any of my current clients again…"

My father held his hand up to stop Maxwell from speaking any further. "Careful what you say next, Mr. Brexley, unless you are certain this conversation is for sure not being recorded and that it may never be played back and held against you at a future date. Otherwise, by all means, go ahead and throw your threats around aimlessly."

Maxwell gave a heavy grunt, knowing my father made a valid point here. The last thing Max wanted to do was to give us Bettencourts any ammunition to hold against him and his family in future litigation, which sounded inevitable at this point.

The luncheon was continuing to be a disaster as Maxwell and my father never ceased to bash each other, while Jasper and I remained silent, watching the entire spectacle with our eyes peeled open, not wanting to blink and miss a single beat.

But my bladder was starting to kick in. After a full glass of the Willett, my seal was about to break and there was no use in me trying to hold it in any longer. Pushing my chair back, I rose up, prompting Maxwell and my father to both stop their chat to glance over at me.

"If you'll excuse me, I need to use the bathroom," I informed them, before trotting off to the nearby public restroom that was right around the corner from the dining quarters.

Once I emerged out of the hall and into the bathroom, I let out a heavy sigh of relief as I stepped into the stall to piss. I wasn't sure whether I was exhilarated to be out from that pressure cooker of a meeting, or rather relieved that I was able to face Maxwell Brexley in person for the first time in nearly a decade and didn't seem bothered or overly fazed by it one bit, despite my ever-growing attraction to a man that was sex personified.

But I needed to put a lid on this boiling pot of steam. I would be a fool not to remind myself of how horrible of a person Maxwell is. He was a vile monster to me when we were at Amplestone Academy. And watching him and my father verbally attack one another back and forth proved that he hadn't changed at all since I last saw him.

As I finished zippering my pants back up, I heard a loud click come from the entrance of the bathroom, like a door being locked. Flushing the toilet, I came out from the stall and peeked around, surprised to see no one was in here with me. *What the hell was that noise then?* I thought to myself.

But I shrugged and disregarded it, stepping forth to the marble sink to wash my hands. Once I was done, I grabbed a towel to dry off, and the second I glanced up into the mirror to gaze at my reflection, one of the bathroom stall doors behind me flung open.

I spun around abruptly, bracing my hands against the edge of the sink as I watched a man who came out of the stall lunge forth at me. He gripped my wrist and threw me against the wall. My back slammed into it, the impact leaving me startled, and practically blacked out for a second. Opening my eyes, I felt a hand reach around my throat, pinning me still.

Maxwell had a diabolical grin on his face. The beautiful demon that he was, showing off that glistening white smile of his. "Well, well, well. This is déjà vu all over again, isn't it, Ace?"

The tension he held on my neck lightened, allowing me to speak. It was then I noticed his ring that was now firmly pressed against me. The band was silver, with an ornate black onyx stone in the center of it. Pitch black like a never-ending abyss.

I struggled to get free, but stood no chance against his godly strength. "Let me go!" I demanded. "Or I swear to God I will scream and sue your sorry ass!"

It obviously wasn't the words he was expecting, nor cared to hear. He made that apparent by tightening his grip around my throat once again, while his other hand now covered my mouth to keep me hushed. "You won't do it. I know you won't. Secretly, you want this. I watched the way you stared at me. You can't resist me. Can you?"

The arrogant asshole! How cocky could he be!?

But he wasn't wrong. Not even close. Maxwell was right. My body and mind weakened whenever he was around me. At first, I thought I was only this way when I was younger. Teenage hormones and all. But now, I realized it was so much more than that. Those same feelings and yearnings I once had by being in contact with him combusted in me like a vibrant set of colorful fireworks. I was submissive to Maxwell Brexley, and the worst part about it was that I was coming to terms with the idea that I desperately needed to be beneath him, both physically and situationally. I couldn't rationalize why, but the feelings were unavoidable at this point. He held this power over me that I had no clue how to overcome.

"And if I recall, you couldn't contain yourself back then. You had to kiss me. And I have a feeling you won't be able to contain yourself now. Will you?" Maxwell added with an arched, curious brow.

Just like that, he released me and stepped back, putting more space between us. I was rendered motionless, shocked that he was freeing me and presenting options before me. But Maxwell knew what he was doing, the slick and sly imp that he was. There was only one option I had. One that my brain, heart, and cock all had made up their minds on the second I saw him.

And so, I dove forward into Max, lips desperate to meet his. My hands wrapped around his neck to bring his head down to me. Our kisses were sloppy at first until we found our rhythm. Then, they remained dirty and untamed, like a bear just coming out of hibernation, ready to savagely maul and eat whatever it could get its hands on.

Maxwell returned my kisses. His hands reached to pull my suit jacket off, before he tugged against my dress shirt, untucking it so that he could reach to feel my soft skin underneath. The touch of his fingers was not as I remembered from years ago. His hands were now seasoned, more weathered and rougher, with slight traces of callouses that I could feel tracing against my sides and back. And I loved it. I craved those hands and fingers on me. I wanted nothing more than to have every surface of my skin exposed to him. A road map for his fingers to navigate and get used to. After all, my body would be their claimed territory now.

But Maxwell's hands reached out from under my shirt and made their way up to my shoulders, putting intense pressure on them. He was pushing me down. Our lips separated, and I was forced onto my knees, my eyes gazing up at him in wonder.

He removed his black leather Hermès belt and unbuttoned his pants, pulling them down with his underwear in a single swoop. My attention darted straight ahead at his massive, girthy cock that was directly in line with my face.

I'm not sure why I glanced back up to look at him. Perhaps part of me was seeking his permission or approval, yet I already knew what I was expected to do. I wanted to wrap my hands around his shaft, to stroke him off, make him feel good. Maxwell had so much pent-up stress and aggression. He deserved to have it all released, to reach that point of ecstasy, where it all would be dispersed from his body. And I needed to be the one to help get him there.

But I didn't even get the chance to squeeze my hand around his dick, feeling his massive palm caressing the back of my head. He thrusted the tip of his cock against my lips, and I was forced to have to open my mouth to receive it. Thrusting ferociously, he penetrated my mouth. The shaft of his now slippery cock slid against my warm, wet tongue, gliding back and forth across my soft lips.

I gagged as I felt him nearly hit the back of my throat, to which he slowed his pace. But the second I had gathered my breath, he viciously pressed the back of my head into him harder, forcing me to gag again. The cycle repeated. My eyes were watery, on the verge of tears from how intense he was, yet I couldn't tap out. I needed to withstand how uncomfortable this was for me. It was my mission to please Maxwell Brexley at this moment. I would not be satisfied until he shot his warm, milky load in my mouth and down my throat.

"Fuck yes," he nearly whispered with assertion. "This is what happens when your father fucks with me, Ace. I then fuck his son. All the aggression he brings on me, I'll send it right back your way. You're my fucking toy now. My little sex voodoo doll. Understood?"

So humiliating. So dirty. So fucking wrong.

But I gave in. My body and mind were submissive to Maxwell, and so I nodded.

"Good," he replied, before he resumed fucking my mouth mercilessly. After a few more minutes, he came into it. His cock pulsated wildly against my tongue, and I tilted my head back slightly, anticipating his salty cum to burst inside for me to swallow.

"Fuck yeah, Ace! Swallow it all! Good fucking boy!" he commended me, like some obedient pet dog.

And I swallowed it hard so that he could visibly see my Adam's Apple contract through my neck as the proof he needed to know the deed was done.

Once my mouth separated from his erect cock that was slowly softening, the height of my sexual appetite digressed now that it was quenched. Reality began to sink in. I felt ashamed. I was weak and disobeyed my father. I was ruining the Bettencourt family name by letting this Brexley own me in this way.

A sudden escape of laughter erupted from Maxwell. I looked up at him, confused. He placed his hand over his face and shook his head like a villain who was bored by something so pathetic that they couldn't be entertained by. "You're all mine, Ace Bettencourt. All fucking mine! I'm glad you were able to get all those years of rest and peace you needed away from me. Because now, you're not going anywhere. Welcome to your very own version of hell."

Chapter 11

Ace

(Age 25)

What had come over me earlier today?

Was I hexed, or even possessed, by some witch?

Did I need counseling?

Should I seek out a therapist?

How could I be so obsessed with this... onyx demon?

My mind was a whirlwind of unanswered questions. I thought I understood myself so well. Metacognition was never an issue for me. I completely knew how I would think and I could predict how I would react to every situation that could ever arise, that is until the situation of Maxwell Brexley came along into my life.

How was it even possible that I could be so sex-craved and mad over the most horrible human-being on the face of the planet? I knew Maxwell was heinous and diabolical. I knew that I should never associate with or even be near the man. But there was something that kept drawing me to him now. An invisible rope that had us attached at opposite ends. Slowly, we were being pulled closer and closer together.

But the only difference was that Maxwell was the one doing all the pulling. I was the sucker that got dragged along for the ride. He held all the control, and he damn well knew it. I was his *fucking toy* as he so lewdly put it when I was on my knees in the company bathroom, servicing him.

That cocky look on his face as he looked down upon me while he fucked my mouth would be ingrained in my mind for a lifetime. But it wasn't just your typical cocky look. There was something so menacing behind it, so wicked. Recalling the scene over again in my head left a curdling feeling in my gut. I wish I could somehow wipe it clean from my memory, to forget the very moment in my life where I was at my weakest. A victim to the prowler that knew how to pull my strings like the marionette that I was to him.

Despite my current disappointment with my poor lapse in judgment by being the gudgeon of my sworn enemy, I could not deny the intensity that burned within me from our bathroom encounter. I've had boyfriends in the past I have had sex with on numerous occasions. But never have I felt the need or the urge to spring across the room towards them to yank the buttons from their shirt and pants off, desperately craving and needing their dick to be inside me. Never had I sat across a table from someone while the area around my groin simmered like a boiling pot of water because of their proximity to me. Never had I been so sexually frustrated and dependent on anyone in my life than I now was with Maxwell Brexley.

The man was now my kryptonite, and I feared how I would react the next time we were around each other. The most depressing thing about this was the unpredictability of it all. I could no longer trust myself when I was in his presence. It was the thing that I dreaded most about our next rendezvous, whenever that may be. And yet, at the same time, it was the thing that would keep me awake at night, wildly anticipating when I would see Maxwell again, *hoping* that it wouldn't be a long intermission until then. Because now that I had the full taste of the elixir that was Maxwell Brexley, it would leave me with an unquenched thirst that could never be fully satisfied by anything else but him.

But I could recognize that my constant wonderings about Maxwell were unhealthy. I needed a distraction, something that could eclipse my every thought about him. Luckily, my father called for a family dinner at his estate this evening. That is, if you could even call it a family dinner. More like a business debrief from the events that transpired today. It was a way for him to inform Leo of all that occurred at the luncheon and for us to strategize our next plan of attack against the Brexleys. Although, who was I kidding? The scheming would strictly involve Magnus and Leo as it always had. I would just sit silently on the side, listening in on their every word, pretending to be fully engaged and often nod my head, so they felt like I agreed with most of their ideas. And tonight would be no different than the other *family dinners* we've had over the years. Or at least, I thought nothing would break our typical family dinner routine.

Magnus remained at the head of the freshly glossed, blood-stain colored dining room table in our family mansion. The Chinese Rosewood table was custom made, and the man probably spent more on it than I cared to even know.

Leo and I sat in the middle of the table directly across from one another, so that we both were on either side of our father. It was another tradition that remained in effect for years after my mother died. Actually, our seats remained this way for as long as I could remember. The only difference now was that at the latter end of the table, the seat was empty, and it would always be empty, since it was where my mother would sit. And as long as I was in this home and we had any guests over, I refused to allow my father to have any of them sit there. Now, what he did behind closed doors was none of my business, and I highly doubted he made the effort to keep it open and available to people when I wasn't around. But so long as I was present, no one would be seated there. It was a non-negotiable, and these were the one set of terms I made that my father never questioned, and always abided by.

Every time I glanced to my right at that empty chair at the end of the table, I couldn't help but grin, remembering my mother's graceful, demure poise. Her warm smile that was contagious and her friendly winks she would often sneak and give me when no one was looking, as we all ate and were engaged in conversation over an extravagant meal. I wanted that memory to remain with me forever, and I could not allow it to ever be tarnished by the sight of someone else there.

Soon, our wine goblets were filled by my father's butlers and the food brought out by his house staff. The dinners he had made were enough to feed a party of twenty, despite there only being the three of us here. My father was a man who liked to have many options. Even food was no exception to that rule.

As we began to imbibe and eat, Magnus was already glancing over at Leo, not wanting to hesitate any longer to fill him in on the luncheon with the Brexleys. "Cocky son of a bitch. That will be his greatest downfall… that ego of his."

Talk about the pot calling the kettle black.

"Or his stupidity in general," my brother added. "The man seems like the only things he is interested in are fast cars, hookers, and white-lines."

So presumptuous. Maxwell was far from stupid. The other things that he was accused of being interested in... not so sure about.

"But you would be insolent to underestimate him, Leo. He is a Brexley, after all. Even a snake is capable of passing its blood to its offspring," my father replied. "Maxwell should not be discredited. Both of you would do well to remember that. The second you think you have the upper edge over your opponent is the very same second that they will come in for the kill."

I nodded while Leo chimed in again. "Yeah. Yeah. Yeah," he scoffed. "I already pulled Toshima away from him. All I need to do is find other cracks in his relationships and deals with his other major clients and I'm sure I can swindle them too."

Swindle? Is that what we were doing?

I thought Leo acquired Toshima Enterprises under clean terms. But was he really swindling Grigory Toshima? I thought he struck an authentic deal with the man, one that the Brexleys could not compete with. Now, I was second-guessing my father and Leo and their so-called *deals* and whether they could uphold the ends of the conditions they offered up to clients or not.

I felt my hands begin to clench into fists beneath the table. Why was I getting so bitter and upset about this? I knew my father to be a con man on the occasion. And Leo followed right in his footsteps. Yet, I never reacted this way before. Was it because they were now hurting Maxwell and his business? Is that what was causing me to become so angry? Because it was now personal, with Maxwell being involved?

"It shouldn't be too hard for you to find," Magnus responded. "If there's a dent in one of his contracts, there's likely to be dents in many others. I need you to move fast on this, Leo. Find a way to investigate Qatalyst LLC. Also, investigate their contract with the Gorman Brothers. They have loose lips in their companies. Just find the right person and…"

My fist slamming into the table interrupted my father's plot. His head turned so quickly from Leo to my direction that I thought he had whiplash. My brother, too, raised his gaze to me, wondering what the sudden outburst was all about.

"I can't do it anymore!" I exclaimed. "The lying, the cheating, the stealing. Why does everything have to be so unethical with you two? Why can't you just play by the rules for once? Why do you always have to resort to deception and dishonesty to get your way? What does that say about the corporation you run, father? Are you lacking in certain…"

But I couldn't finish my line of questioning. My speech, too, was put to a halt by my father, who reciprocated the favor when I did it to him. "You fool! How dare you question my methods, my empire and all that I built!? You ungrateful little shit! This house, this lifestyle, everything around you was all because of how ruthless I've been. It doesn't matter what fucking way I get the job done. The only thing you should concern yourself with is that *I do* get the fucking job done. Come hell or high-water, it happens. The path to get there… Psh!" He waved his hand in the air dismissively. "Who gives a shit about the path? It changes every damn day. What matters is knowing which path to take in order to come out on top. And I've mastered that skill long ago, son. It's a cut-throat business. Hell, it's a cut-throat world!"

Immediately, I regretted my involuntary reaction in calling him and my brother out for their questionable trade actions. I wasn't sure what overcame me, but this was not the end result I intended for. "I... I..." But I couldn't find the words. There was no way of back-pedaling out of this one. I knew I was in for further reprimand, and so I would take my brutal lashes willingly.

"You need to grow a spine, Ace. A fucking backbone! Your mother pampered you for far too long. I warned her..."

It was the lowest blow he could ever give to me, bringing my mother into this.

The fucking nerve of him! The fucking disrespect!

But I had to bite my tongue. It would only end poorly for me if I were any further disobedient. *Nod and keep your head down, Ace. Just like you've always done your entire life.* I told myself. *What's one more dinner in the grand scheme of things?*

Leo didn't utter a single word. His eyes just bounced back and forth between my father and me, like a pinball in an arcade machine, moving in every which direction. I knew he wouldn't dare interfere on this one. Just like when it came to most things about me, he never got involved.

"I too should take part of the blame. I've been far too hands-off with you recently, son. It's time for me to make amends for that and rectify your weak ass. So, here's my proposal..."

Oh god! Not another Magnus Bettencourt negotiation...

"You need to follow mine and Leo's lead. I want you to get chummy with Maxwell Brexley. He didn't seem all that bothered by you at our luncheon. If anything, he was rather tolerable when it came to you. Let this be your test. I want you to infiltrate Brexley Global by befriending the head of the snake itself. If you claim to be so nice, decent, and honest, then it shouldn't be a problem for you to be friends with the Brexley boy, no? Show your true colors. He'll admire that about you…"

What the hell was my father even suggesting!? Had the wine gone to his head that quickly!?

He was going on a tangent now, rationalizing his logic aloud. "You'll do it, son. Because if you don't pull this off, I will pull *you* off of our non-profit organizations. You will have no stake in anything related to Bettencourt Corporation. Furthermore, I'll revoke your entire trust fund and all your accounts."

"But father…" I gasped.

"You can't be serious, dad. I don't think Ace stands a chance of pulling this off," Leo finally intervened, too little too late.

"It's done. I'm not going back on my word, and that's final!" Magnus definitively responded.

And he wouldn't. That was for sure. My father never altered the conditions of any negotiation he's ever made. At least out of any of the ones I was aware of.

My father and Leo probably thought they understood and knew me all too well. That I needed to get my hands a little dirtier if I wanted to survive and thrive in the Bettencourt world. That I wasn't worthy of the Bettencourt title if I didn't get blood on my hands. And they were right on all those counts. But they were wrong about one thing. Magnus thought that taking my money and funds was the worst punishment of all, which wasn't the case at all. I could care less about our millions and this lavish lifestyle I was living. No. The greatest punishment he was invoking was having me removed from leading our non-profit organizations, meaning I would no longer run the Positive ViBes Charity Foundation that was dedicated to my mother. That was what hurt the most. I already had one person detach me from the closest thing I had to my mother years ago. And I couldn't risk it happening a second time, now.

Chapter 12

Maxwell

(Age 27)

The restraint that it took to keep myself from looking in his direction at that fucking poor excuse for a lunch was a bitch. When Jasper and I stepped foot in the Bettencourt territory and I saw Ace at the far end of the dining hall, something hit me. It felt like an asteroid had collided with my heart, a feeling I'd never experienced in my entire life.

But that was put on the backburner once Magnus starting running that hideous fuck-mouth of his. Or rather, it was me that was the one throwing out most of the insults. However, that smug look on his face and his little snide comments and jabs he gave riled me up to the point of no return. My blood burned into liquid hot magma. Magnus knew how to push my buttons and he did a fucking fine job of it.

Our conversation became so heated, I had to get up and walk the fuck off. Otherwise, I would have leaped across the table and pulverized the living shit out of the old goat. The rage in me swelled like a festering wound, ready to bust at any given second. I needed to unleash it somehow, and then I did the unthinkable.

I trailed behind Ace, who left just a short moment ago to go to one of the nearby restrooms. The hall was pretty vacant. After all, this was the Bettencourt private dining quarters specifically meant just for the tyrannical CEO and his business partners and guests. So, I was confident that I could ambush Ace without a soul ever knowing.

For safe measure, I locked the main door behind me once I entered the bathroom. The tinkling noise coming from one of the stalls let me know Ace was still pissing. So, I stealthily entered a stall nearby and shut it. I peeked out through the small gap in the side of the door to get a good view of the sink area. Any moment, Ace would come out and wash his hands. And when he did, I would come out from hiding, ready to pounce on my sweet little prey when he would least expect it.

Pinning him against the wall with my hand on his throat was so poetic. *Fucking. Beautiful.* It had to have triggered those lustful feelings I knew he still had for me. I would never forget how he stared at me nine years ago with that yearning and passion in his eyes. I stirred something within him that I knew no one else could have the potential to do. Maybe it was my cockiness that led me to believe it, but deep down, I knew it to be true.

And sure enough, it didn't take very long for Ace to reveal that my thoughts were right on point. He kissed me like his fucking life depended on it. But I had more in store for Ace than just making out. I absorbed so much enmity from that no-good father of his. Now it was his turn to make up for it.

Ace would drain my cock, help release all that built up fury I had in me. And he would fucking enjoy it. That I was certain of. But never did I imagine I would savor the experience as much as I had. Ace's mouth felt like a warm Dyson vacuum. I've had the occasional blow job from strangers over the years, ones who my assistants forced to sign a non-disclosure agreement to keep fucking hushed over it. Plus, they were paid handsomely as a bonus consolation for doing so. But none of the blow jobs had felt this fucking phenomenal.

I wasn't sure if it was Ace's skills or perhaps the sexual friction we had with each other. After the nearly ten-year hiatus, maybe it was the anticipatory excitement that made it all the more enjoyable. I wasn't quite sure what it was, but nevertheless it was amazing.

Ace was so fucking submissive, just like I pictured he would be. And I could tell he loved to service me. His mind was so fucked, and I was the one fucking it like the sick son of a bitch that I was.

I soon realized the power I had over Ace. He was desperate to have me. And I was there with him. It took every ounce of control in my body not to pull him up to his feet, bend him over the sink and shove my cock right up that delicious ass of his. But I couldn't reveal my cards to him just yet. I had to show him who was the boss in this toxic, bizarre relationship that existed between us. So yeah. I spewed out some alpha, domineering shit to him, calling him my *fuck toy* and that he was *fucking mine*. I think I even called him my personal *sex voodoo doll* somewhere in there. At any rate, he got the picture that I was the one in charge and his mission was to do whatever it fucking took to please me. And it ended with him guzzling and swallowing my cum down his throat, which he obediently did.

After that intense oral session, I buttoned up my pants, tucked in my shirt, and walked out of the bathroom, not daring to look back. It was a calculated move on my part, but it was the only way to keep Ace thinking he was a worthless cumdump to me, which is exactly what I needed him to think. It would keep his mind fucked and him coming back for more.

Jasper was waiting at the front of the dining hall. So, we gathered ourselves together and took off. I didn't bother to bid farewell to Magnus, and of course Ace, who was probably paralyzed on his knees on the bathroom floor, not sure of what the hell to make of what he did with me. I'd had enough of the Bettencourts in a single day. That quota was full to the fucking max. So, my cousin and I made a clean getaway and returned to Brexley Global.

It wasn't until that evening that I called Jasper back into my office before we left for the night. "What's up, cuz?" he asked, as if I was one of his dim-witted college frat brothers. He took a seat across from me with another cigar dangling from his mouth.

"You know, I've been thinking… after our meeting with Magnus and his pet son," I began.

Jasper scratched his chin, wondering where I was going with this. "Yeah? What about it?"

I laced my fingers, folding my hands together as I leaned forward onto my desk. "Magnus is fucking impossible. He won't cease the petty little games he plays with us, no matter what. We'll just have to bite the bullet for a bit longer and deal with it."

"Yeah. I wish that old fart would just fucking croak already," my cousin added.

I shrugged his comment off and continued with my train of thought. "We should be focusing our attention elsewhere. We need to play with the endgame in mind. It's only a matter of time before Magnus is out the door. So, really, we should be striking deals and getting chummy with his spawn."

"Leo and Ace?" Jasper raised a quizzical brow.

"Yes. Unless there are other little bastards that he spread his sperm to, which wouldn't fucking surprise me. But we should be looking into ways to speak to them privately, to get familiar with them. Hell, maybe even let them think we're friends with them or some bullshit."

"So, what exactly is it you're proposing?"

"Let's invite them out for a boys' night. We could host a poker tournament at my penthouse. We'll bring Cecil along to, to keep them intimidated. What do you think?"

Jasper smirked at the idea. "I mean, it's worth a shot. Do you really think they'll take us up on the invitation?"

I couldn't help but chuckle at the thought. Of course, Ace would take the bait. There was no way he would pass on an offer to get the chance to see me again. I was damn sure of that. "Yeah. I know for a fact they will."

Sure enough, it wasn't even twenty-fours later that I learned from one of my personal assistants that Leo and Ace would be willing to partake in the poker tournament I had planned for us on Friday night. However, they requested that we accommodate a *plus one* they planned on bringing. Immediately, my mind jumped right to their father, Magnus.

Christ! Did he have that tight of a fucking leash on his sons!?

Magnus coming would defeat the entire purpose of the event. I might as well cancel the whole damn thing if he was planning to join. But much to my relief, my assistant informed me that the person they wanted to tag along was Kent Scythe. Instantly, I recognized the name. The real estate tycoon himself, who had an agency and brokerage empire under him. Based on gossip I've overheard and some of the social media outlet news stories I've come across, I also gathered that he was a total playboy, with a new guy's arm wrapped around him every week, practically.

I was surprised that the Bettencourt brothers kept him in their company. Ace and Leo were nothing like Kent. The only thing they had in common was their wealth and being high up in the business world. Well, that, and the fact that Kent and Ace were both gay, too. Leo, I wasn't so sure about. However, it had been years since he had a girlfriend. Still, there was something off about him that left his sexuality partly questionable.

At any rate, despite Kent Scythe being a notorious power bottom, I was much more pleased that he was the plus one they intended on bringing, instead of Magnus. And because of that, I told my personal assistant to let them know that it was fine for Kent to join.

So, I realized it would be an even playing field. The Bettencourts had Ace, Leo, and now Kent. On the Brexley side, we had me, Jasper, and our friend and *fixer*, Cecil, who worked for my father and for me now. Cecil was a silent, but deadly man. When threats needed to be made, and we had slimeball clients who weren't holding up their end of our contracts or tried to fuck us over, Cecil would *take care of them*. Had the man ever killed anyone? I was pretty damn sure he had. But he kept his own personal and business affairs to himself. It was best Jasper and I knew nothing about how he ruined the people that fucked us over. Less of a mess for us to handle. Plus, litigation and all that fucking jazz. Despite his seedy background and stone-cold personality, he was a close friend and ally of mine, one of the few people I could count on my hand that I trusted in this world, which is why I liked having him in my company whenever I was at a social gathering or event of some sort.

Tonight, he entered my penthouse with a gun in his holster, tucked away behind the gray suit jacket he was sporting. I had a hunch other weapons like knives and sorts were somewhere hidden on his body as well. "Thanks for coming, Cecil," I greeted him with. "I hated to pull you away from whatever plans you had tonight, but could really use your support here."

He gave me a solemn stare. His emotions and reactions were always unreadable. "No problem..." was all he simply stated before bypassing me. It wasn't the first time Cecil had been in my penthouse, so he knew exactly where my formal study was, where we had the poker table set up. A bartender stood behind the onyx bar counter in the room with plenty of drink options, while a young female server would wait on us for the evening.

I watched as Cecil headed straight for the bar, patting Jasper on the shoulder, who was in mid-conversation with the bartender with a drink already in his hand.

It wasn't for another thirty minutes that the Bettencourts and Kent arrived. Leo was in a typical suit that was usually a shade of orange or brown he often wore, matching his copper-colored hair. Tonight, it was an amber-toned one. Kent wore an all-white blazer and dress pants. Did he think this was some fucking *Saturday Night Fever* audition or something? And then there was Ace. I was expecting to see him in a formal outfit just like the others. But no. He wore a tight black V-neck shirt that hugged his toned biceps, chest, and abs nicely. His slim, dark designer denim jeans made his quads and ass pop. And based on the red bottom soles on his shiny black dress shoes, I knew they were Louboutins.

This was a side of Ace Bettencourt I was not used to. Who knew he was that fit and had all of that hot body hiding underneath his suits? I had to remember that this was now Ace, all grown up and not the scrawny little teenager I met almost ten years ago. He definitely came into his own, and I had to admit this Ace before me left my dick already rising to half-mast.

I did a quick sweep with my eyes over his full body subtly before drawing my attention back up to his face. I gave him a sinister grin, tapping into the role of being the arrogant, cocky asshole that he wanted to own him.

To the rest of them, I would do my best to come off as sincere. And so I politely greeted them. "Welcome to my home, Leo and Ace. And this must be Kent Scythe. A pleasure…"

Kent held his hand out, offering for me to shake it, which I reluctantly did. "Thank you for having me, Maxwell. I must say, I've only ever seen your picture online and those images barely do you justice." He gave me a wink after his compliment.

Was Kent hitting on me? Of course he was. He was the biggest man-whore in the city. I shifted my gaze over to Ace, who was slightly biting his lower lip. I imagined he felt uncomfortable with his own friend flirting with me, which I absolutely reveled in.

If I was out of the closet, I would have easily wanted to make Ace a little jealous and have him squirm a bit by witnessing me flirting back with Kent. But me being gay was still a kept secret. Therefore, I just nodded and remained unfazed by Kent's remark. "Anyway, let me give you all the short tour of the place before we head to the study for the remainder of the evening."

And so, I escorted them throughout my 18,000 square foot penthouse. It wasn't until we arrived at the kitchen that I noticed something was slightly amiss with Ace. Out of my periphery, while I was talking to the three of them collectively, I noticed him trace his hands along the edge of my black onyx kitchen island, so intricately. He seemed to be in a daydream as he moved about the room. The clueless look he held on his face was so mesmerizing. Him and his hot body, the sexy outfit he had on, plus the way he was moving up against my onyx kitchen counters. I would be lying if I said it didn't turn me on and leave me imagining my dick plowing into his ass while his back laid on the countertop with his legs raised and ankles resting on my shoulders.

"But why is everything black?" Kent curiously asked, bringing me back down to Earth. "It takes a certain person to put up with a dark kitchen. What's your reasoning?"

Leave it to the real estate expert to question my interior design taste. Honestly, it was none of his fucking business. On a normal day, I would have foul-mouthed him and have one of my security guards escort his sorry ass out of here. But my mission was to make the Bettencourts comfortable around me, enough so that hopefully the more we hung out, the more they could trust me and would be wise to never try to pull the same shit their father does against my company in the future. And that required me to be as amicable as possible with them, despite how every nicety I made sent a disturbing inkling feeling crawl beneath my skin.

"Black symbolizes power and mystery. It's always been my favorite color. And then black onyx… there are so many layers to an onyx stone," I informed them.

"Are there many layers to you, Brexley?" Kent further inquired.

I nodded. "I guess you could say that. There is more to me than meets the eye. Yeah. I put on a pretty tough and hard fucking front, but you'd be surprised at what you'd find when you peel back the layers."

Ace's eyes widened a bit when I stated this. Something about what I said must have captured his attention and resonated with him. God, I wanted to climb into that weird mind of his and see his exact thoughts.

"So, you'll find that a lot of my furnishings consist of black onyx. Call it my signature look or something like that," I added.

Kent raised his hands in the air in defeat. "Still, not good for the resale value. Most people look for light and bright kitchens, not ones that look like they belong in the Underworld."

"Well, lucky for me, I don't plan on ever selling this place. Why sell something I don't need the money for? Hell, by the time I die, I want at least one-hundred homes across the fucking world."

This garnered a laugh out of Kent. Even Leo slightly chuckled at the comment. But Ace remained silent, just staring at me with a puzzled look on his face.

Yeah Ace. I'm giving you a million different sides to me. Good luck trying to figure me out.

Fuck. Now that I honestly thought about it, I wasn't even sure if I fully figured myself out yet.

Chapter 13

Maxwell

(Age 27)

It seemed that I was getting docile Ace tonight, yet again. As we finished the tour of my place, I had everyone gather in the study. Cecil and Jasper were already seated at the poker table. Their conversation halted the minute they saw the Bettencourts and their loud-mouth friend enter.

Pure silence for the next several seconds. A stand off. A stare off. Whatever it fucking was, you could cut the tension in the air, even with a dull butter knife. I decided to intercede to make the situation less awkward for everyone.

"Why don't you three grab a drink from the bar?" I suggested to Ace, Leo, and Kent. "Just come to the table when you're done and I'll make introductions."

All three nodded and traipsed over to my bartender while I moved to the poker table to give Cecil and Jasper a demonic glare. "Are you two fucking kidding me?" I whispered.

"What do you mean?" Jasper asked.

"We're supposed to be making them feel comfortable. Befriending them. Instead, you two stare them down like they're your next fucking meals!"

Jasper shrugged. "Sorry. I couldn't help it. Just seeing them here irks me. I'll get over it soon and change my attitude. Promise."

"You better!" I gritted my teeth, threatening him. I then glanced over at Cecil, who seemed lost. Was he even paying attention to me? His eyes were locked in on the three of them at the bar. Once I turned to see where exactly his focus was, it was actually on Kent.

Jasper also noticed his inattentiveness, causing him to wave his hand in front of Cecil. "Yo! Earth to Cecil. What the hell, man?"

Cecil swatted his hand away, but then clenched Jasper's wrist hard, nearly crushing it. "Don't do that again," he warned.

"Christ! Okay. Chill!" Jasper responded, before he was able to retract his hand from Cecil, rubbing the aching sore.

"Shhh! Here they come," I spoke under my breath, as Ace, Leo, and Kent strolled over our way with their drinks in hand. Kent and Leo had bourbons on the rocks, meanwhile Ace held the stem of a glass filled with red wine. He was the only one without a bourbon, whiskey, or scotch. It stood out like a sore thumb.

"So… do we have assigned seats or what here?" Kent blurted out like the high-maintenance little fucker that he is.

Was I over-analyzing the room or was everyone here completely on edge but me? Which was ironic in itself. I made a mental note to myself for future get-togethers. Micro-dose all drinks and cocktails to make these fuckers relax a bit more.

Jasper and Cecil still weren't talkative much. They were as useless as a fucking giraffe trying to swim in the ocean. I realized I would have to take matters into my own hands and be the lively mediator for the evening. "Yes. We will draw for seats. But first, Ace, Leo, and Kent… meet my cousin Jasper, and our friend Cecil. Jasper and Cecil meet Ace, Leo and Kent."

Everyone at least had the fucking decency to stand up and exchange handshakes with one another. As I watched everyone's initial encounter, I couldn't help but take notice of Cecil and Kent's interaction with each other. Cecil held Kent's hand a little longer than the others. The eye contact they made with one another was rather bizarre, too. Both of them were stiff as a board. It made me wonder if they already had met before or knew each other prior to this. Something was odd about the whole thing. I would be meaning to ask Cecil about it later, but I would need good fucking luck with that. Prying personal information from Cecil Astor was like having a shitty, spoiled toddler get its haircut for the first time. He would squirm non-stop about it, and you would have to come back on a different date to try again later.

While everyone was now up and out of their seats, I decided to address Kent's earlier question. "So, if everyone's now ready, we'll go ahead draw cards for seats as I mentioned. Lowest card will sit here," I patted the chair in front of me. "Then, we'll go clockwise with the next lowest card and so forth. Any objections?"

Everyone's silence was my cue to continue on. As I explained the rules, the antes, the blinds, and timeframe we would use to raise blinds, the poker dealer I hired came over, sitting in the center of the table facing us, to disperse everyone's chips and shuffle the cards. "Standard Texas Hold'Em tournament rules apply, gentleman. Any questions or are we good to get started?"

No one spoke up, letting me know to proceed. "We are all ready, Albert," I informed the card dealer, speaking for the group.

"Alright. Small and big blinds. I'll take your bets, then I'll hand out the hands," Albert instructed.

Soon enough, the tournament was underway. Finally, everyone could now drink and be merry around each other while we played. At least, that's what I was hoping. And for the most part, that's exactly how things proceeded. Jasper and Leo were hitting it off pretty well. But they had that *second fiddle to a brother slash cousin* trait in common, so I should have expected them to have an unspoken bond based on that in itself. Kent was being deafening and obnoxious just as he had the minute he stepped foot into my penthouse. Cecil remained silent as always, scanning the table, trying to get a read on everyone. But I could hear a few gruffs under his breath whenever Kent made some irritating comment.

But Ace Bettencourt was still the tough fucking nut to crack out of anyone. I should have expected it though, right? We shared a secret that no one else at the table was privy to. He was probably scared shitless about it getting out to anyone and figured that staying quiet this whole time was his best and only option. Not to mention he was damaged goods now that I had him wrapped around my fingers. Ace probably had no idea how to react in front of me. He hated me. He lusted for me. He despised me. He craved me.

Poor sexy little fucker was a whirlpool of mixed emotions. And for some reason, that turned me on so much. He was submissive and obedient, but at the same time, trying his best to stand his ground and hold court.

The more drinks I had into the tournament, the less control I seemed to have with keeping my eyes off of him. His spiked up dirty blonde hair was flawless and every time he swayed his hand through it, it made my cock leap. Those crystal blue eyes of his were so focused on his cards during every turn, I couldn't help but get lost and entranced by them. I wanted those eyes to widen when he would feel my dick plunge into him, Ace taking every fucking inch of me. What I would give to tell everyone here to fuck off and get out of my study, except for Ace. Once we would have the privacy, I'd pound his brains out right here on the felt green table. It would be my hands sweeping through his hair and yanking on it, while I fucked him like my life depended on it.

It wasn't until Cecil kicked me from under the table that I came back to reality. He gave me a disturbed yet stern look.

Shit! Was I that obvious in checking Ace out?

I shook my head, diffusing those thoughts, before glancing back down at the card table. The *flop* that showed on the table was a three of hearts, ten of spades, and ace of clubs. Ace had raised a higher bet over my big blind, while everyone else had already folded. Meanwhile, I had pocket aces in my hand giving me a three of a kind.

My eyes scanned over the cards on the table once more and then back up to Ace who held his gaze on me, wondering if I would call his raised bet. Of course, I would. Only a fucking idiot would fold on a three of a kind at this point. I had the best possible hand on the table.

"I'll call," I declared, pushing my chips towards the center.

The dealer then flipped over the *turn,* which was a queen of diamonds. Instantly, before I could even react, Ace had pushed his full stack of chips towards the middle. "All in!" he enthusiastically announced. It was the most spirited I had seen him all night. Hell, in my whole fucking life, for that matter.

I eyed him up suspiciously. The only way Ace could have a better hand than me would be if he had a jack and a king in his pocket, which would give him a straight. But I doubted this was the case. After all, he was making aggressive bets well before the queen appeared, which would only then have given him the straight.

Ace played a conservative game all night so far. Yet, I wondered if that was his strategy all along, to play it safe and make the rest of the table believe him when he would eventually make bold bets in the later phase of the tournament.

Yet, I was confident in my hand enough to go against him. I had to see if the brave fucker was bluffing or not. And if he was, I would make him pay for it by trying to lie to me. I'd smack his ass so hard when we fucked, I'd make sure there was a permanent red handprint on both of his smooth ass cheeks for the next month to remember his punishment by.

"I'll call that," I responded, further pushing all of my chips into the center of the table too. The dealer had to count both of our stacks out, in which he gave Ace a small stack back in return, meaning he had just slightly more money than I did.

"Yeah!" Kent yelled. "Finally, some action here! It's been a snore-fest so far."

Cecil just rolled his eyes at him.

"Alright. Go ahead and turn them over, gentlemen," Albert instructed.

And so Ace and I revealed our hands. I spread my pair of aces in front of me while he smirked, showcasing his king and jack.

Lucky fucker!

I beat my fist into the table, aggravated as hell.

He made those aggressive bets just to hope for that fucking queen to appear, which it did. So, he had a straight, and I had a three of a kind going into the final card, the *river*, to be turned over by the dealer.

Everyone was on the edge of their seats as Albert flipped it over. And it was an ace of hearts.

"Fuck yeah!" I shouted, realizing I now had a four of a kind, beating Ace's straight. The other guys at the table roared, shocked a fourth ace had popped up for me in a single hand. Even Ace was stunned. His mouth hung open, and he was speechless. I couldn't help but picture my cock thrusting into that perfectly circular gape he now had.

"Holy fuck! Poor Ace," Jasper chimed in with. "Tough luck, man. I've always said that Maxwell was born with a horseshoe up his ass." This managed to get a chuckle from everyone at the table, including Ace, who held his hand over his mouth to try and hide his snickering.

"And don't any of you fucking forget it!" I added.

I couldn't help but give Ace a devious grin. The irony of this hand wasn't lost on me. I held two aces, just as I had Ace in the palm of my hands. And then more aces revealed themselves on the table in my favor. Ace was now fully giving himself to me. I couldn't have written anything more fucking poetic.

Everyone stood up and stretched out after that exciting hand. I could see most of the glasses everyone was drinking from were near empty. Now would be as good a time as ever to call for a break. "Why don't we all take a brief intermission? Feel free to use the bathroom, get some refills, and then we can reconvene in about ten minutes. Anyone opposed to that?"

"Sounds good to me," Leo responded, while everyone else nodded their heads in agreement.

"Perfect. And if you need to use the restroom, one of my assistants at the door will point you in the right direction if you've already forgotten where it is," I informed them.

Most of the group beelined for the bar to get more bourbon, while Ace was the only one who walked in the opposite direction, towards my assistant who waited at the main door. I watched as she pointed her dainty finger, giving him directions to a private bathroom. As soon as he exited the room, I trailed behind him.

As I approached the bathroom door, I could see the light was on beneath the crack of the closed door and hear rumbling within it, letting me know he was in there. Too bad for me that it was locked from within, since it was a single bathroom. There was no way for me to bombard Ace like the last time. Instead, I played it cool and leaned seductively against the black damask wallpaper across from it.

When Ace opened the door, I caught his eyes widen with alarm at the sight of me. "Having a good time, Ace?" I inquired, with a shrewd smile.

He stood in the doorframe, still for a second, trying to process what I asked, before he tried to scoot by me without saying a word.

But I wouldn't allow it. I held both of my hands against the wall near him, trapping Ace in between. "I asked if you're having a good time…" I repeated, this time not so endearing.

He shrugged, keeping his head turned to the side, refusing to make eye contact with me. "Yeah. I'm okay, I guess."

His lack of emotion vexed me. I understood this game he was playing and I knew it wouldn't end well for him at all if he kept it up. That, I would be sure of.

I pressed my body froward. Our hips were barely inches apart. I tilted my head to the side to whisper in his ear. "Just *okay*? I'm sure I can fix that," I uttered, purposefully blowing my warm breath into his ear. "I am the host, after all. So, tell me Ace. What can I do to make sure you're having a *great* time?"

I was toying with him, and it was too fucking easy. Yet Ace wasn't taking the bait as easily as I had hoped. "You don't need to do anything, Max. I'm fine. Now, if you'll excuse me…"

He pushed my arm out of the way, but I was quick to grab his wrist before he could walk off back to the study. There was no way I was letting him go. Since the blow job he gave me, I'd been dying for the chance to have this one-on-one time with him again. And now that the time finally presented itself, Ace wanted to play hardball and ignore his own carnal feelings?

Absolutely. Fucking. Not.

I wouldn't allow it. My hand gripped harder on his wrist, pulling him into me so that we were chest to chest. "I have a lounge room down the hall. Come with me. I'll lock it behind us and throw you against the chaise and give you all that I know you fucking want. Don't try to fight this Ace. I know you want it just as bad as I fucking do."

Instead of taking me up on the offer, he violently pushed me away from him. "No! I said I'm fucking fine. What part of that don't you understand, Maxwell? I may have been weak and in a vulnerable state at the luncheon when I last saw you.

But that's not me. You don't get to hold any power over me anymore. We're no longer at Amplestone. We're not some dumb hormone-driven teens any longer. So, grow the fuck up!" And with that, he turned his back toward me and stomped towards the study.

I was rendered paralyzed, shocked that Ace had turned me down. I was fucking Maxwell Brexley. Millions of men and women would grovel and make so many fucking sacrifices just for the chance to have sex with me. And I knew this to be true because of the many sordid DM's and pictures I've received from complete strangers over the years. Yet Ace shut the opportunity down instantly.

Just when I thought I had Ace Bettencourt all figured out, I realized there was more to the little shit than meets the eye. I should be angry. I should be beyond fucking pissed for not getting my way with him. Yet, I felt none of that. A new feeling erupted within me. One of fascination. What was it about him that fucking did this to me?

I placed my hands over my face with irritation, becoming aware that the tables were turning. Ace was growing a backbone finally, or rather maybe he already had one, but I was too fucking cocky to be able to notice it. Nevertheless, I couldn't just let Ace move on. I hadn't even had the chance to fully fuck him yet. And what kind of a top, apex predator of the food chain would I be by letting one of my prey escape from my clutches?

Chapter 14

Ace

(Age 25)

I put on the most stern expression I could muster up when Maxwell approached me in his hallway after I came out of the bathroom. It wasn't until I could avoid his advances, turn my back to him and walk off when the sigh of relief finally escaped from me. Hopefully, Maxwell bought the entire act.

This whole night turned out to be one long-winded performance. First, I filled in Kent Scythe on all that had transpired between Maxwell and me earlier that day at my luxury condo. We sat in my bedroom, planning the details of this evening. Despite his extraverted personality, Kent was someone I could trust. After all, I had way more dark secrets on him than anyone else, having been friends with him over the past ten years. He was mischievous as hell. So, if he were to divulge or leak my and Maxwell's relationship to anyone, Kent would have so much greater to lose. It wasn't a risk he would ever be willing to take, for sure.

When I first told him about Maxwell Brexley being gay and hooking up with me, he could not help but bust out laughing. "I knew it! There was no way a guy that hot could go that many years without being married or let alone in a relationship." Then, once he unleashed all of his opinions on Maxwell's sexuality, then he came after me. And Kent aimed straight for the jugular.

"Really Ace? Of all people to fall for, you're going to fall victim to Maxwell Brexley?"

I crossed my arms over my chest. "What do you mean?"

"I expected a naïve, middle-class twink to fall for Maxwell. Hell, anyone on Earth that wasn't you. You are strong, rich, and powerful. Above all else, you're sweet, kind, and don't deserve to have to deal with... *that*."

I grunted in disappointment, agreeing with everything my friend just threw at me. "I know! He is a monster, yet I can't help it. Even knowing that, I am just drawn to him for some reason. Maybe it's our history together? I don't know. There's just something about him, Kent. I'll never figure it out."

Kent came up to my side and patted me on the back. "At least we know one thing for sure. You are definitely into him. There's no denying or even avoiding that. But we have to find a way to change the roles up here, Ace. If you keep going down this current path, he'll never take you seriously and just keep using you as his little fuck toy. Do you want to be Maxwell Brexley's mere fuck toy for the rest of your life?"

Now, I will say, there were so many people that only *wished* they could be Maxwell's fuck toy. I was certain of it. But I was not one of those people. Yes, I wanted to make love to him and give into him sexually, but that was the extent of it. I didn't want him to be rude and cruel to me at every given hour of the day. And Kent hit the nail on the head. I deserved so much better than that.

"No. Of course not," I admitted.

"Good," Kent replied. "Then, if you do want to try to see where things go with him, you need to take a stand. Give him an ultimatum."

"But he will flat out turn me down and away if I did that. I don't even think he wants to be in a relationship or anything like that."

"Well, we don't have to give him a verbal ultimatum. Give him a psychological one," Kent stated.

Now I was confused. "What do you mean by a psychological ultimatum?"

"I mean, refuse him. Turn down all of his sexual advances. I'm sure the playboy isn't used to it. He wouldn't know what the hell to do with himself. If he moves on and finds other tricks to use after that, then you know he was always broken and not worth the trouble. But if he really does want you and fights for it, then maybe there's a chance that he is salvageable after all," Kent elaborated. "And I know it's going to be hard for you to not give in to Mr. Sex God, but you don't really have a choice here, unless you want to be treated as his trash for the rest of your life."

"No. You're right. I have to stop playing into his games," I confessed.

"Damn right you do," Kent then stood up and moved across my bedroom to my walk-in closet. "Now, we'll have to decide what you should wear tonight. He'll expect you in a suit and tie like the rest of us, but we're going to throw him for a loop. Keep him on his toes… Oh, and now knowing he's secretly gay, I'm totally going to flirt with him and make him uncomfortable as hell. Let the mind games with Maxwell Brexley begin!"

The walk from the hall back into Maxwell's study was so difficult for me. I did everything I could, everything that Kent had advised me to do when I would come face-to-face with Maxwell at his home. Now the ball was in his court. I took my position, and I dug my feet deep into the sand. He knew my stance. It was his turn to make a move.

But Maxwell Brexley was more unpredictable than British weather and I had no clue as to how he would react to my refusal of his sexual proposition to me. That was what petrified me the most. Would he just brush it off and move on with his life, or would he find a way to meet me halfway? If he completely discarded me altogether, what then? I would always wonder *what if* for the rest of my life, never knowing what it was like to feel Maxwell's fully exposed body up against mine. What it would feel like to have him make love to me, to have him immersed and buried deep inside me. I craved that feeling more than anything else. It's what drove me to be so sexually submissive to him. The confidence and power he evoked. It was so beautiful in some sick, demented way.

So. Fucking. Beautiful.

It crushed me to turn him down. I could have had sex with him right then and there in his lounge, spread out on his chaise. Yet, I turned down the deal with the onyx demon. And I now had to handle the consequences of that decision, no matter how hurtful they may be.

As soon as I returned to the study, I noticed that Kent, Leo, Jasper, and Cecil were all seated, ready for the next round of the tournament to begin. I knew I needed to get the hell out of here. There was absolutely no way I could sit here in silence any longer and just have a stare down with Maxwell Brexley, especially not after the encounter we had just had. I couldn't bear the thought of having to look at him in the eyes at any other point tonight.

So, I rubbed my stomach, pretending as if I was coming down with something. "I'm not feeling all that well," I informed the group.

Kent and Leo gave concerned looks to me.

"Do you need medicine or anything?" Leo asked. "I'm sure Maxwell has something you can take."

I shook my head. "No. I don't think I need to take anything. I just need to lie down. I think I'm going to call it a night, guys. Sorry for being the first to go."

Jasper smiled. "Oh! Don't worry about it. Do you need to say goodbye to my brother before you head out or…"

I intervened. "No. I'll just send him an email or something."

Kent then rose to his feet. "Well, do you want one of us to come home with you?"

What was it with these guys? Just let me go home alone, please.

"No. I'll be fine. You and Leo should finish the tournament. I'll send for another driver to come get you two," I implored.

"Okay. Take care of yourself," Kent replied.

"I hope you feel better," Jasper added.

"Thank you. We'll have to do this again sometime," I said, before turning around to walk out of the study.

Luckily, Maxwell had yet to return, which was perfectly fine with me. Now was my chance for an escape. I wouldn't have to run into him again, which I would be completely hopeful for.

I needed time to process this entire thing. I wasn't quite ready to tackle it head on. What would I say to him now? Nothing. That's what.

So, I navigated the halls and to the front foyer. The second my hand reached for the door handle, I heard my name being called out.

"Ace, wait!" someone shouted from behind me.

It was the voice I dreaded to hear. I closed my eyes, lowering my head, when I immediately recognized it. Why I stopped and froze, I'll never know. But there was no stopping whatever it was that possessed my body to remain still and not bolt out of the penthouse.

Maxwell was approaching me. I could hear his footsteps against the marble floor, closing in the distance between us. I refrained from turning around still. It wasn't until I felt a hand softly squeeze my wrist that I reacted in a hostile way, shaking it away from his touch. Although, I knew the way he had grabbed me this time was more placated than any other time I had ever experienced him touching me. Still, I was on edge from his most recent physical aggression with me. And so, I acted belligerently. "What Maxwell!?" I practically yelled. "What more could you possibly have to say to me?"

"I'm sorry, Ace. I'm not sure what came over me. Maybe I took it too far?"

"You think so?" I said, sardonically.

"Look, I'm no good at these sorts of things. I honestly thought this was what you wanted. I thought you were enjoying this whole *game* we're playing. Or whatever the fuck this is between us," Maxwell replied.

"It's not a game, Maxwell. We are real people, with real feelings," I informed him, as if he were some emotionless golem who didn't have a soul. "And what is going on between us now, it's not what I want at all. I deserve better than this. I deserve someone who can give me so much more."

"I know… I realize that now, which is why I'm apologizing."

It hurt me to my core to see this side of him. It was a side to Maxwell that no one else probably had ever seen in their life before. I was afraid to turn around and look him in the eye. Would I then tear up? Would I kiss him for taking the next step in apologizing to me? I couldn't be so forgiving just yet. That would only make me seem weak still. Yet, I could not trust myself to not turn around and leap into his arms like some star-crossed lover.

"It's going to take more than an apology to right the wrongs you've done to me, Maxwell. It's going to take a hell of a lot more than that."

And so, I turned the handle to open the door before walking out on him. Now, I was confused more than ever. I had no idea what the future would hold for me and Maxwell Brexley or even if a future existed between us. But when the crisp night air struck me in the face, as I made my way out of his building and into the black car that waited to take me home, I felt alive. I was no longer numb. And because of that, I felt my lips curl into a smile.

Chapter 15

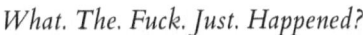

Maxwell

(Age 27)

What. The. Fuck. Just. Happened?

Ace had just flat out denied me. I couldn't believe it. He wasn't seduced by my charm, my looks, my power, none of it. Never in my life had someone refused anything I had to offer them.

It was the absolute worst fucking feeling in the world. My heart sank into the deepest pit of my stomach. I'm not sure which was worse, the fact that I was rejected or the thought of me being completely wrong in reading this entire situation with Ace.

He was completely into me. He had to have been. I scrutinized the way he looked at me, like I owned him when we kissed and when he sucked me off. There was a longingness in those oceanic eyes of his. Their waves trying to withstand the songs of the Sirens. But I was his fucking Siren. Ace was so fucking infatuated with me and submissive. There was no way he could turn away from me. At least that's what I had thought all along, up until this point.

Ace withdrew his hand from mine and returned back into the study. I sat on the honey leather settee in the hallway, needing to regain my composure to process what had just happened. I was in shock, unsure of how to navigate this situation.

A fucking first.

Ace was no longer fazed by me. The spell I had him under had dissipated and apparently, he really was no longer the weak, scrawny kid I remembered at Amplestone, just as he had referenced before he stormed off.

The Ace Bettencourt that was in my presence now was strong-willed and able to withstand even the greatest of power and temptation. And that was something to be admired. Who else could fucking have the nerve to turn me down? No one. That's fucking who. Never has a man or woman ever shut down the opportunity to be with me.

Maybe I was going about this in all the wrong ways. I shouldn't have come on so strongly in our first few encounters we now had with each other as adults. Perhaps I should have eased my way into my dominance over him. Maybe if I was a little more kind and subtle around him, I could have gotten the chance to fuck him, and then resort to my savage ways once we got into the bedroom.

But now, I honestly wondered if I had ruined those chances of ever getting the opportunity to bed Ace. No. That was un-fucking-acceptable. That couldn't be the end all be all. I could backtrack from this. I just needed to be honest with him about why I acted the way I did.

Be honest with him.

I gulped and cringed at the very thought of it.

But did I really have a choice? It was the only way I could salvage this entire fucked up scenario I had created. For now, I would have to rejoin the group in the study and put on a fake, undisturbed face and pretend none of this ever happened, until I could somehow manage to get Ace by himself one more time to explain myself. But that seemed like it was becoming more and more impossible. After what had just transpired between us in this hall, there was no way he would isolate himself from the group and take a risk of being ambushed by me again.

My prey was learning fast. Stay with the herd and never go astray, or face the consequences of being targeted by your predator. Ace was learning this quickly, much to my disliking. Or was he?

I suddenly heard the sound of footsteps striking the marble floor, heading towards the front door of my penthouse. I rose to my feet and sprinted to the foyer, wondering who was trying to leave in such a hurry. Although, the second I asked the question in my mind, I realized I already knew the answer to it. Who the fuck else could it be besides him?

My suspicions were confirmed as I approached Ace, with his hand on the door, ready to hightail it out of my place. I called out to him and luckily; he remained still.

He. Fucking. Stayed.

It was then that I knew I had a fighting chance to correct things between us. And so, I laid it all out on the line. I spilled out my guts. My words coming up like uncontrollable vomit. I even fucking apologized to him, which I only had ever done a handful of times in my life.

But it wasn't good enough for him. Not even fucking close.

"It's going to take more than an apology to right the wrongs you've done to me, Maxwell. It's going to take a hell of a lot more than that," were the last words he uttered before he departed.

I was left standing all alone in my foyer, confused as ever. What were all these wrongs I've done to him, besides wanting him to be my sexually obedient plaything? Unless he was still harboring onto what I did to him ten years ago at Amplestone with that lion that belonged to his mother. But he still couldn't be holding onto a grudge like that for that long. Could he?

It had been a full two weeks since the poker tournament. Life went on as it normally did, in the sense that I went to work six days a week, nearly ten hours a day, and stayed busy, keeping Brexley Global afloat at the top of the business world totem pole. The only thing that was new was the added stress level I had as a result of things ending on a sour note with Ace. Not once had we communicated since that evening when he stormed out of my penthouse. But why would I expect him to reach out? He made it quite fucking clear he wanted nothing to do with me until I made amends with him.

But I had no clue as to how to go about and even do that. Plus, it wasn't in my nature to come begging and groveling to anyone, even if it was Ace Bettencourt. As much as I was to blame for shit hitting the fan between us, he would still need to meet me halfway if we wanted to press forward. Not that I even knew what *pressing forward* meant for us and our relationship.

Did I want to be in an actual relationship with Ace? Fuck no. I wasn't some domesticated animal who could live that sort of lifestyle. I've never had a boyfriend in my life. Hell, I wasn't even out of the closet yet, so what was I expecting? And more importantly, what did Ace think could happen between us? All I knew was that I wanted to be intimate with Ace and no one else. That much I was certain of. But anything beyond that, I couldn't picture. It seemed like it was in the realm of impossibilities.

However, to even be intimate with Ace meant that I still needed to try to work things out with him, if I wanted to make that happen. But I couldn't just reach out to him right away. I wasn't that immature. Ace needed some time to breathe. Some time apart from me would do us both good in the long run. We had kept our distance from each other for ten years already. What's an added few weeks or even months in the grand fucking scheme of things? Yet, I would soon realize that this timeframe I had in mind on when I would next see Ace would actually be completely out of my control.

Tonight, I was having dinner at my parent's mansion. A bi-monthly tradition that has been ongoing since I graduated from college. My sister Charlotte and I were expected to be prompt and arrive no later than 5:00pm on the first and third Saturday of every month. If one of us had another major commitment at the time, then the rain check date would always be the following Saturday.

Needless to say, Topper and Victoria Brexley were strict with this rule. There even was a time or two when Charlotte and I were threatened that breaking this tradition would only cause our parents to take us out of their wills, remove our inheritance, and cut the cord on all credit cards and financial obligations they supported us with. And being the spoiled fucking brats that we were, we never missed a dinner. Of course, we couldn't risk losing that lifeline.

As of last year, my father invited Jasper into the mix. And so, the five of us now sat in my parents' formal dining room. Salads and appetizers were before us, with three different glasses above our plates. One for water, one for red wine, and the other for white wine.

The table and silverware were finely arranged thanks to my mother's obsession with maintaining the same etiquette as a Victorian queen would.

Of the offspring at the table, I was the most prim and proper, compared to the social Neanderthals that were Jasper and Charlotte. My sister constantly tried to sneak her phone out beneath the table to check her text messages and social media. It was so blatantly obvious when she did it, too. My mother called her out at least five times during every one of our dinners. Meanwhile, my cousin had the vocabulary of a derelict with the overuse of words in his frat boy lexicon like *dude*, *yo*, *bruh*, and *cuz*.

I cringed at nearly every sentence he spoke.

I'm not going to lie. Sometimes, I was just as fucking irritated with them as much as my parents were. But tonight, the stars aligned in a different pattern. Topper Brexley would be pissed off at someone else besides Charlotte or Jasper.

"As you all know, our annual Brexley Charity Gala is coming up in two weeks," my mother informed all of us. "I'll need all hands-on deck with the set-up and logistics."

The Brexley Charity Gala was our company's main event of the year. Over five hundred invitations were sent out for attendance. Some celebrities and CEOs had to make calls to my mother just to get in. Others resorted to making even larger donations than in previous years just to remain on the guest list. And this year, the competition to get this invitation for the elite would be no different.

Although, little did my mother fill us in on a secret she'd been keeping that would make this year's gala unlike any others in the past. "Also, things will be slightly different this year. We are taking another charitable organization under our wing."

My father seemed more caught off-guard than anyone at the table by this announcement. "Another charity? Do our donors know this? Are they okay with it?" He voiced his concerns.

My mother gracefully nodded, swirling the remainder of her red wine in the bowl of her glass. "Of course, Topper! Do you think I'm incompetent?" The question was obviously rhetorical and my father knew damn well to keep his mouth shut and not answer it if he wanted to avoid the wrath of Victoria Brexley that our family had only seen a handful of times. But nevertheless, we knew it existed, and no one dared to disturb that monster that slept in its cave.

"So, what organization will we be collaborating with this year?" I inquired.

"The Positive ViBes Charity Foundation," my mother nonchalantly replied.

Both my father and I rose to our feet, as if our chairs were on fire and they had burned our asses. Our eyes both widened with horror at what my mother had just revealed to the group. Jasper and Charlotte just stared at one another, unsure of what the hell was going on.

"You mean to tell me we are partnering with the Bettencourts!?" My father's face turned beet red. The vein popping from his forehead became more prominent.

"Yes, dear. Over a week ago, Ace Bettencourt, who runs the Bettencourt charity organization, reached out to me. He admired the charity I built for our family and sought out my advice and expertise. The darling boy was charming, to say the least. He is nothing like that mediocre father of his. Anyway, I was more than flattered by his interest. After all, this is all for charity. So, I offered to take him under my wing. And so, he agreed to partner with us at our gala," my mother elaborated.

I was speechless. Who knew Ace had it in him to be able to pull this off and let alone have the fucking balls to actually admit his shortcomings with his own charity and reach out to a Brexley for support. I wasn't sure whether to think it weak, foolish, or even admirable. For some reason, I found myself leaning towards the latter.

My father slammed his fist against the dining room table. "Victoria! Are you out of your ever-loving mind!?" he shouted. "How could you think that partnering with a Bettencourt would be okay? The boy is just using you and your kind nature. Can you not see right through him?"

She crossed her arms, disappointed at my father's remark. "I think you are being overly insecure, Topper. Believe me, I saw no ounce of Magnus Bettencourt in his son, Ace. The boy is nothing like his father in the very least. He just needs a little help with growing his own charity a little. The Positive ViBes Charity Foundation is in honor of his mother, Vira, you know?"

Topper was livid. He was not used to his wife contradicting him. "I still can't believe you aren't questioning his motives. I refuse to allow this to happen. I won't be caught dead at an event that we are co-hosting with the Bettencourts." My father then shifted his attention over to me. "Why don't we let Maxwell decide? He is the CEO after all, and gets the final say. So, what do you think, son?"

He held a devious grin on his face, a grin I often recognized when I sometimes looked in the mirror at myself. It was uncanny. But my parents were putting me in a tricky spot right now. One of them would walk away pleased, while the other would likely resent me for whatever decision I made.

Charlotte and Jasper sat on the edge of their seats, eying me with wonder. It was the most excitement they've ever experienced at a family dinner. Hell, it was the most dramatic dinner any of us have been a part of together.

My eyes darted back and forth between my mother and father. Eventually, I let out a heavy sigh, ready to give my final verdict. "The Bettencourts have plenty of social connections that we can take advantage of if we were to partner with them. I see it as a smart business maneuver."

Victoria was elated, while Topper scoffed with disappointment. "Horrible move, son. You're going to regret this. And I won't be there to pick up the pieces. Now, I'm actually regretting handing you over the company this soon. This is beyond weak of you, Maxwell."

My father turned away and excused himself from the dinner table, trekking off to some far corner of the mansion.

Topper hit right where it hurt most. But I knew he said it out of spite and didn't really mean it. I was similar to my father in that regard. When someone made a rude comment or went against us in some way, we were quick to take a stab back at them, harder and deeper, so that it hurt them far worse than it hurt us. Call it a defense mechanism I learned from him over the years.

But I had lost my appetite now. I threw my napkin down on the dinner plate and walked off, too. On any given day, I would have rejected the proposition of working with the Bettencourts in any shape or form. Yet, I saw this as an opportunity for me. An opportunity to make amends with Ace. This was my one and hopefully only olive branch I would have to give him. I was going out on a limb here for him, going against the better judgment of myself and my father. And if Ace wasn't willing to finally accept this branch, then I'm not sure what else I could do, because this was the only branch I think my ego could possibly take and give.

Chapter 16

Ace

(Age 25)

Clink.

"Here is to the end of a crazy long work week!" Kent clinked his champagne glass full of Dom Perignon against mine before we tossed our heads back to take a sip of it.

"The end of a crazy long work week?" I repeated back, stunned that he toasted to that of all things. "Those don't exist for us. We pretty much work 24/7 and are on call, no?"

Kent chuckled. "I guess you're right, but just go along with it. Don't ruin the moment, Bettencourt."

The two of us sat on the cushions of a lounge sofa in a private section up on the rooftop of Salon de Ning in Midtown, overlooking the glorious, brightly lit metropolis full of tall buildings and skyscrapers. Both of us dressed to the nines in our dapper blazers. Kent's was a quartz white color, while mine was royal blue.

It was a last-minute text I sent him today, asking if he was interested in joining me for drinks tonight. But Kent would be quick to cancel any and all plans just to hang out with me. Others would have to wait days, weeks, or even months just to receive a personal call or text from real estate mogul, Kent

Scythe. But his best friend and fuckboys (can't forget them) were the only exception to this.

Tonight, it was important that we met up. It was getting down to the wire with planning the charity gala I was co-hosting with Victoria Brexley. I needed to fill Kent in on this and personally invite him to it, sooner rather than later, in case other plans were on the horizon for him. I could really use his support there.

"So, I'm not sure if you are aware, but the Brexley's annual charity gala is next weekend," I announced.

"Yeah. It's a total snoozefest. I went once three years ago. Met a hot guy there and brought him back to my place that night. That was the only highlight of the evening. The only saving grace."

I couldn't help but lose my stern expression and bust out laughing at his brazenness. "Well, I hope you're not bored with it this year, because I'm going to need you to join me in attending."

The perplexed look on Kent's face said it all. I could practically see the cogs in his head spinning. "Wait, what? You received an invitation to the Brexley's charity gala? How the hell is that even possible?"

"Because I'm co-hosting the event with Victoria Brexley," I finally revealed. "The Brexley's charity organization is partnering with Positive ViBes. It was me that took the initiative to have a sit down with Queen Victoria herself. I was brutally honest with her, and wanted her guidance in building our charity organization, since I'm new to the world, compared to her. She was very open and receptive to the point where she offered to include me in running the gala with her."

"Wow!" Kent had to take an extra-long sip of champagne in order to digest all that I had just told him. "Hell really must have frozen over."

I nodded. "It would seem that way. Victoria is nothing like Topper and Maxwell. Clearly, she must have seen that I was the apple of Magnus that rolled very, very far from the tree to a whole other orchard for that matter."

"Well congratulations! This event will definitely put Positive ViBes on the map. Hopefully, you'll get a ton of donations and regular donors to be active sponsors," Kent added.

"Here's to hoping!" I raised my champagne glass in the air to meet his, which he obliged. We clinked them together once more.

"Oh! You know I wouldn't miss it for the world. Especially an event where the Brexleys and Bettencourts are all in attendance. Are Leo and Magnus joining?"

"To my knowledge, yes. Leo and Magnus are expected to attend any and all of our charity organization events, no matter what crowd," I informed him.

"Interesting." Kent rubbed his chin with his palm, almost diabolically. "So, this will be your first time actually seeing Maxwell since poker night, then?"

"Yes. It will be." I took a long swig to finish my champagne before reaching for the bottle of Dom Perignon in the ice bucket beside us to refill my glass.

"And?" He paused, expecting me to finish his thought, but I had nothing to say.

"And what?" I asked.

"And… what are you going to do when you see him? Are you actually going to forgive him this time around? Do you think he will apologize again?"

"Woah. Woah. Woah. One question at a time, please," I playfully requested. "First off, I'm going to be cordial when I see him. It is a charity gala after all. Tons of people will be there. The last thing I would want would be for someone to catch me being angry or rude. It would be off-putting, and I can't risk losing potential high-stake donors. Secondly, I'm not sure if I'll forgive him. What has he done since that poker night to make me forgive him? Nothing. So, unless he has some amazing speech planned that will sweep me off my feet, then I doubt I will be able to forgive him."

And a small part of me wished something like that would happen. Everybody dreams of being *that person* who can change a demon into an angel. We secretly want to be the reason a bad boy makes a change and learns from his ways. I was no different. A helpless romantic to the very end. But I was also no fool. Maxwell Brexley wasn't your typical rough around the edges, bad boy. There was such a complexity to him that would even make Dr. Phil cry in trying to diagnose it. And because of that, I didn't hold on to high hopes that he would come around and work to be kinder to me and try to fix the damage he had caused, both recently and in the past.

I never did forgive him for what he did to my stuffed lion, Gabriel. Only a sinister and evil person could ever do something so cruel. Even when I mentioned to him that it was the closest thing I had to my mother, he never even bothered to bring it up. Not once did I ever receive an apology from him in the ten years that followed. And I would never dare bring it up to him.

It wasn't my job to make him see the error in his ways, to force an apology out of him. He needed to see it for himself, for it to truly be authentic in order for me to actually fully forgive him for all the turmoil he had put me through.

A long pause ensued after I thought I had answered all of Kent's questions. But he then reminded me I missed one of them. "You didn't say whether or not you think he will apologize to you again. Do you think he will?"

I simply shrugged. "I honestly don't see it happening. When you have an ego that big, and it gets bruised, you'll think to never make the same mistake again twice."

Chapter 17

Maxwell

(Age 27)

The charity gala of the year. What everyone thought was the most lavish and entertaining event every single time it was held was merely a fucking bore-fest for me. Of course, being CEO of Brexley Global, I didn't have much of a choice in deciding whether or not I wanted to attend.

Yet, this year I felt so differently about it, all because of Ace Bettencourt. The fucker was more on my mind than I cared to admit. He wasn't just your typical gay rich boy, heir to a mega-conglomerate, like someone who should be partying on yachts in the Mediterranean and lounging on the white sands of Mykonos in a sexy speedo. No. There was so much more to Ace that I was slowly unveiling. He's also not a mere pushover who grovels at my feet like all other men. There was a newfound spunk to him that I never knew existed. I should feel the need to destroy him for this behavior. But even I was now wavering. Despite this, he still remained a mystery to me. And that enigmatic side to him was what was keeping me engaged.

Now, here he is canoodling with my mother, running a joint charity foundation party with her, against his better judgment and likely against the wishes of his own father. Evidently, Ace didn't care what anyone thought, and that's what was also driving me fucking mad about him. The courage, the bravery, the similar *I don't give a fuck* attitude I possessed. Ace was starting to eat away at me, and I was realizing there wasn't much I could do about it.

I stood at the bottom of the white marble stairs, just outside the gala, staring up at the building. A plush red carpet was rolled out, surrounded by stanchions to block the public and paparazzi from intruding. The flashbulbs were going off like crazy. It was enough to give me a fucking migraine. Then came the arms stretched out towards me with microphones in their hands.

"Mr. Brexley, how does it feel to be named the most eligible bachelor in the city?"

"Tell us, how is it being the most powerful man in media?"

"Rumor has it there's a new woman in your life."

"Is it true? When do we get to meet the lucky lady?"

"Mr. Brexley…"

Ugh. Enough already. Relentless little fuckers. I bolted up the stairs and into the main event hall, escaping the flashes and commotion. Although, once I proceeded into the dining hall, I was once again bombarded by other nosy people who were attending the event. Major donors and people who had ulterior business motives trying to get their one-on-ones with me to make pitches and propositions. I had made it out of the frying pan and into the fucking fire.

The second a waiter rounded me, I reached for the champagne flute on his silver tray. Alcohol would be my best friend if I was going to make it through this charity fundraiser without going the fuck off on someone.

While stakeholders were gabbing, I couldn't help but tune them out. I had other priorities on the forefront of my mind that were proving to be a distraction. Specifically, trying to pin-point where Ace was. Yet, there was no sign of him.

Eventually, it was my mother and father that came up to me to steer me away from the business talk.

"You look dapper as ever," my mother greeted me with in her ruby Stella McCartney dress, planting a light kiss on my cheek that left the slightest trace of a faded scarlet lipstick stain.

"Fetching as always, mother." My eyes glanced over her shoulder at my father, who had a stern look on his face. Clearly, he wasn't all that pleased to be here. And I couldn't blame him. Especially, after his entire family went against his wishes by inviting the Bettencourts to this event. The man felt defeated and likely on edge with his enemies getting a free pass to roam into his own territory.

"Father, how are you this evening?" I sincerely asked, hoping to diffuse the tension in the air between us.

"As well as I'll be, I suppose," he coolly replied. At least this was a start.

I reverted my attention back to my mother. "And where is your co-conspirator?" It was pretty fucking blunt and to the point, but I couldn't control my sweltering emotions. I just needed to see him and I had no more time to stall.

"Oh. Ace Bettencourt?" She glanced over my shoulder around the room. "I'm not quite sure. He's probably greeting guests, dear."

Not the answer I was looking for, but it would have to do for now. Any further line of questioning in regard to the Bettencourt boy would likely raise skeptical red flags in my mother and father's mind, making them suspicious over why

I was harboring on Ace was out of the question. I didn't need that hanging over my head.

"Well, I have to go make more rounds, as I'm sure you do too," I informed them.

My mother agreed and conceded. "Yes. Our table is in the front, per usual. I'll see you in a little while. And Maxwell? Do be on your best behavior. You know how much this event means to me," she genuinely requested.

Did my mother not fucking know me? Or rather, she did, which was why she was imploring this. But she should know I could put on a brave and proper face without causing any mischief. I would just have to blame her innate maternal instincts for still treating me like a child at times still. Brush it under the rug.

"I promise that I will behave, mother. See you in a few…" And with that, I made a quick dash out of there and towards the nearest bar. A stiff drink was exactly what I needed. A bourbon on the rocks. As I retrieved my glass from the bartender and turned to face the main floor, I finally caught sight of Ace, with a bright glow about him. His smile was radiant as he greeted guests, hugging some while shaking the hands of others. I could tell he was in his element now.

He looked so damn fresh in his tight gray suit. His dress pants tugged at his glorious leg muscles, showing off his sexy, toned curves leading up to that beautiful ass of his. Needless to say, the drink I held in my hand was no longer the only stiff thing on me at the moment.

Before I could make my way over to him, an irksome voice beside me at the bar drew my attention. "I was expecting a bit more this evening, seeing as how everyone raves about this gala every damn year. But it's rather dull and underwhelming."

I turned my head abruptly to see that the source of the insult was none other than Magnus Bettencourt, much to my annoyance. The man was on my shoulder like a fucking tick.

"That's rich coming from you. I've heard those same words used to describe your performance in bed," I jabbed back.

It garnered a vexed grunt out of the old bastard. "Throw all the immature comments you want at me, Brexley. At the end of the day, we both know who holds more power here. I could wipe your company dry with some of the shitty contracts you've made recently. Don't think I'm not aware of the greedy deals you've negotiated. All it takes is one of my plants to whisper in clients' ears about what Bettencourt Corporation could offer them and they'll go running for hills, just as Toshima did."

I don't know what it was about this man in particular, but he always managed to spike my internal body temperature. I could practically feel the flames burn on the inside of my body, just by listening to him.

"What do you want, Magnus? Can you show a little respect, at least for tonight? Your son is partnering with my mother to make this event happen. Even I'm lowering my barrier just for tonight, all to support your Positive ViBes Foundation, and that's fucking saying something. Do you not see that?"

Magnus threw his hand in the air, scoffing my comment off. "Smoke and mirrors, my boy. You Brexleys are all the same. Clearly, you have caught on to how weak my son is. He is easily manipulated, and naïve to a fault, which is why you practically poached him to collaborate in this event. Get in the boy's good graces only to squash him when he least expects it. We're all cut from the same cloth. Don't think I've never done the same to people before. But little do you know that there is more to Ace than meets the eye."

Yes. There is. Something I've said many times about him, myself.

"Perhaps you are letting your guard down with him too soon," Magnus continued. "At the end of the day, never forget who his father is. I know my son inside and out. I know all the chords to pluck on him and I will always be the one who he listens to when all is said and done. My opinion of him matters to Ace more than anything else in this world."

It took every nerve in my body to control my fist from being raised to throat punch the shit out of this geriatric tool bag. "Have a good evening, Mr. Bettencourt," I mustered up, before walking off. I needed to get out of this claustrophobic nightmare I was in. I needed air.

Fresh air. Fucking. Immediately.

I made my way over to the large white French doors at the end of the hall that led to the balcony. It was currently off limits to everyone, everyone except me, that is. Nothing was off limits for me. So, I could give a rat's ass of the minor blip of a consequence I could face by walking into a prohibited space. I slightly opened the door ajar and snuck my way out onto the balcony, hopefully as stealthily as I could, without anyone paying much attention to my actions.

Once I felt that draft of the breeze strike me in the face, I knew it was just what I needed. I could already feel my head start to clear up. My thoughts could finally run free, their prison cell door finally opened.

It sickened me to hear Magnus talk about Ace in the way he just did, as if his son was nothing more than a fucking puppet to him. Ace doesn't deserve it and Magnus sure as hell doesn't deserve this loyal and devoted son that he was getting. I couldn't help but think about the future and what it possibly held for me and Ace.

I knew one thing for sure, though. If I wanted Ace in the picture, it would have to be without his father, Magnus in the frame. I could barely tolerate the man for more than one minute in a setting. How the fuck would I manage to deal with him for even longer, especially if I had intentions of being around Ace a lot more?

I needed to find a way to cut the umbilical cord that Magnus still had attached to his son. The fucking leech that he was. If only there was something I could find on him that could be enough of a concern for Ace to sever ties with his father altogether.

As if on cue, Cecil Astor came up from behind me. "Is everything okay?" he checked with me.

"Yeah. I just needed some fresh air," I explained. "Listen. I need a favor from you."

"Name it," was all Cecil uttered. A slight chill ran up my spine at how dark he sounded in saying that. It was as if he was hoping I would put out for a hit on someone, to which he was more than ready for some bloodshed.

"I need you to dig up some dirt on Magnus Bettencourt. A man like that has to have some pretty fucked up secrets from his past. I need you to get me something I could use that would ruin his family. It's time I separate him from his sons, once and for all."

Cecil folded his arms over his chest. I could tell he was disappointed by this request. It was considered *light work* for him. He probably was wishing for something that involved more adrenaline and weapons or something along those lines.

"Does this have something to do with Ace?" he blatantly asked me.

It caught me off-guard. "Wh-What? No. Of course not. Why would you think that?"

"I'm trained to observe my surroundings, Max. I don't miss a beat," he confidently spoke.

I let out a deep sigh, frustrated that I was not more subtle in how I stared and watched Ace from afar. Now I wondered if anyone else had a hunch as to my feelings in regard to him. "Enough in trying to dissect this," I practically demanded. "Can you do the fucking job or not?"

He nodded. "Of course. Give me a few days and I'll be able to report back to you with something."

"Good." I replied.

Seeing as how he realized I was done with this conversation, Cecil turned to head back inside to the party. I spun around to overlook the lit-up metropolis before me, eying the sparkling city that gazed back at me, with its bright, massive skyscrapers. This was my city, my fucking town, and I took so much fucking pride in that. I stood there for a few minutes, awestruck by its gloriousness.

It gave me a moment to reflect on things. To reflect on myself. I had changed over the past month. The whole thing was pretty un-fucking-settling, to be honest. Something, or rather, *someone,* was derailing all of the work I had put in to being the man that I was today. Powerful, cocky, reckless, villainous. I could feel all of it slowly but surely beginning to unravel, and there was nothing I could do to stop it.

The fucking Bettencourt boy consumed me, way more than he ought to. And I had to admit to myself that I've never felt this way about anyone in my entire life. It was a feeling I was not quite used to, one that I was not fully comfortable with possessing. It tugged and ate away at me. It was something I had no idea how to navigate through, and that's what fucking scared me the most.

My train of thought was cut short as a shaken voice called out to me from behind. "Hey. Is everything okay out here?"

My eyes bulged with alarm. That voice... it was the voice I had been waiting to hear all night. I turned to face him. The smoldering, charming man in the tight gray suit stood just a pace away from me. The second I saw him, I could feel more of me continuing to unravel. More of me becoming undone.

Chapter 18

Ace

(Age 25)

"Ace. It's a pleasure," Victoria Brexley greeted me in the main dining hall of the charity gala. "My, don't you look handsome as ever," she stated, observing the gray suit I was wearing.

I went in to hug her, admiring the vision that she was in her stunning red dress with dangling diamond earrings and a matching stunning necklace that I didn't even want to imagine the cost of. "The pleasure is all mine, Mrs. Brexley…"

She cut me off right away to correct my salutations. "Please, dear. Call me Victoria."

I nodded to acknowledge her request. "Very well, Victoria."

"So, what do you think?" She raised her hands in the air to show off the lavish venue.

"It's phenomenal! Better than anything I could ever imagine. I appreciate you being able to take Positive ViBes on as a partnering charity for the event," I thanked her with.

"Of course. Although," Victoria then glanced around to make sure no one was close enough to eavesdrop in on us before she leaned into my ear to whisper. "Between you and me, it wasn't just me that had a say in this partnership. The decision ultimately lied with my son, Maxwell. He agreed to the terms."

This threw me for a loop. Maxwell was the one that made all of this happen? I was still so confused. "What do you mean?"

"Well, my dear. Let's just say Topper was completely adamant against us collaborating with one another. It was Maxwell that overruled his father's wishes. It made for quite the interesting family dinner…"

But whatever else it was Victoria Brexley had said thereafter, I completely tuned out. I was completely distracted by what she had just told me. It was astonishing to think that Maxwell had a strife with his father, all because of me. This whole event was possible, all because of him.

It was the most unselfish thing I had ever heard of Maxwell Brexley doing, and it was all for me. This was his apology to make amends for all that he did to me recently and in the past. It was his redemption tour, and I was turning into his number one fan and groupie on it.

I couldn't help but smile on the inside over it. Max really was coming around. He really did care about me and didn't want to just dismiss me out of his life forever. I was finally able to recognize this now. But how would I approach it? How would I handle myself around him from now on, now that I was privy to this information?

"… Oh, I'm sure I've been talking your ear off!" Victoria patted my shoulder, which shifted my focus back to her.

"Not at all," I fibbed.

"Well, at any rate, I best let you get to our guests. I have plenty of people I still need to greet as well, ones who will be disappointed to have donated thousands of dollars if I don't recognize them at all this evening. Take care, Ace. And I will see you soon when they serve dinner."

With that, Victoria Brexley strode off. She barely made it ten feet before a couple bombarded her to engage in conversation. I traipsed in the opposite direction before I too had Reginald and Diana Peterson stop in front of me. Reginald has been a client of Bettencourt Corporation for nearly two decades now. I politely smiled at him and his wife.

"Reginald… Diana… I'm so happy both of you could make it out tonight," I took both of their hands in mine to greet them.

"Nonsense, Ace. We wouldn't miss this for the world," Diana replied.

I became lost in business talk with the both of them, until out of the corner of my eye, I noticed a tall man standing at the nearby bar. His lustrous black suit and shoes and black undershirt stood out among the crowd. Not that it would stand out to most people, because many other men at the event were also in black, with their penguin tuxedos. But this individual was the only person daring enough to pull off an all-black ensemble at a charity foundation. It was the onyx demon I had been hoping to catch sight of all night.

Maxwell looked so fine, leaning his back against the bar counter with a glass of brown liquor in his hand. The seductive and inviting image could easily be on a GQ magazine cover. The only issue was that he wasn't alone. I could see my father beside him. The two did not look thrilled in the slightest to be talking with one another.

Just what were they up to now?

But I couldn't fully focus on them. I had to continue to make small talk with the Petersons. Within a minute, in my periphery, I could already see Maxwell storm off, away from my father. I followed his every move, which led me to catching him sneak out onto the balcony in the back of the hall. I politely waited a good minute in further talking with the Petersons before I could interrupt them, finding an appropriate stopping point.

"Oh! It seems I've been keeping the Lancasters waiting for a bit too long." I threw my hand in the air and waved, pretending there was someone across the room who had captured my attention. "If you'll excuse me, I still have a few other guests I need to greet. Please, feel free to help yourselves to any and all appetizers, as well as drinks at the bar or the champagne that's going around. We'll catch up again in a little while. Again, I am sooooo glad the two of you could come out tonight to support the foundation. My mother would be delighted."

Now that I made my exit speech, I darted in the direction I saw Maxwell head in, which led me to the double set of white French doors leading out onto the balcony. I opened them and stepped outside, only to see that Maxwell was alone, leaning against the stone knee-wall overlooking the brightly lit up city, sipping from his glass of what I assumed to be whiskey or bourbon.

I couldn't help but express my concern aloud to him from seeing him leave the party to come out here so suddenly, like he was irate about something. "Hey. Is everything okay out here?"

Maxwell spun around, with a shocked expression on his face. He was no doubt surprised to see me out here on the veranda with him. "Yeah. I was just getting some fresh air. That's all." There was a lightness in the tone of his voice. Usually, it was deep, cold, and seemed angry all the time.

"Oh. Okay." Silence lingered a bit longer. This whole situation was awkward. I wish this tension between us was non-existent.

After taking a sip from his cocktail, Maxwell broke the ice once more. "I hope the event is to your liking?"

I nodded. "Yes. It's more than I could have asked for. I appreciate your mother being able to offer her assistance and guidance."

"Of course. My mother is a saint. She's always willing to lend a helping hand," he said, almost as a matter of fact.

It stunned me to witness this calm Maxwell that was before me. I wondered if he had been like this around everyone recently or if it was an effect that I strictly had on him. Secretly, I hoped it was the latter.

"Yes. Your mother has been an absolute blessing. But I don't have her just to thank. I am grateful for all that you did too, to make this happen."

"Me?" Maxwell raised his brow at me. "I haven't done anything that needs thanking. This is all yours and her doing."

I shook my head. "You don't need to be modest, Max." It was a line I thought I'd never hear myself say. If I were a gambling man, I would have bet a million dollars that those words would have never come out of my mouth in a lifetime about Maxwell Brexley. Clearly, I would have lost that bet. "Your mother informed me of what transpired at your family dinner. That it was your father who was against involving me in the charity gala. Yet, you were the one that trumped his decision and allowed it to happen."

"It seems like fucking blabbermouth is another title I need to add to my mother's repertoire, besides *saint*," he quickly added.

I couldn't help but lightly chuckle at his response before I became serious once again. "I'm sorry, Max. Had I had any clue that this partnership between your mother and me would have caused angst among your family, I would have never agreed to it."

Evidently, this was not the response Maxwell was looking for. Actually, it seemed like he was disturbed by this entire conversation altogether, for he instantly turned back around to face the city, holding his head down in shame, not wanting to look me in the eyes.

"This whole thing is embarrassing," he announced. "I don't need your thanks. I don't want an apology from you, Ace. If anyone should be giving an apology…"

But I could not allow Maxwell to finish that sentence. I stepped toward him, reaching for his hand. I held it in mine. At first, he flinched, but then squeezed my hand tighter as he turned to face me. I could feel the impulse that traveled between us as our skin touched. It was as if his heartbeat was racing at the same beat and rhythm that mine was, so that the two were completely in sync. I could tell he sensed it, too.

"You've already apologized to me," I reminded him. "Plus, this entire event… it's more than enough for another apology, Maxwell."

He smirked at me, but then immediately glanced over at the French doors that led back into the spacious dining hall. He retracted his hand from mine, quickly. We both had gotten so lost in the moment, we had nearly forgotten that there was a whole party full of people inside. All it took was one person to catch sight of us holding hands to cause a scandalous news frenzy. And Maxwell still was not out of the closet.

"Why don't we start over?" I suggested.

"Start over?" he repeated, with a curiousness in his tone.

"Yes. Why don't we now call the playing field even? Let's clean the slate and maybe have dinner together? Casual, of course. Just two new friends getting to know one another. What do you say?"

Maxwell erupted with laughter, placing his hand over his face. I was perturbed by his sudden hysterics.

"What's so funny? Do you not want to do it?" I asked.

"No. Of course, I want to have dinner with you," he explained. "It's just… I don't know. I will never understand you, Ace Bettencourt. The way you think. The way you feel. It's all just one giant mystery. And I'm beginning to realize it's hopeless for me to even think that I can solve it."

His response elicited a smile out of me. "Well then, don't overthink it. I'm not some opponent of yours. You don't have to try to get into my head and trace my every thought and predict my every move. Just go with the flow."

But as I gave this piece of advice to him, even I realized that perhaps I should take note and listen to it. Because deep down, I too wanted to get into that messed up mind of Maxwell's. I wanted to change it, warp it, and allow it to be freed to see the brighter side of the world. A world that Maxwell Brexley was not quite used to.

Chapter 19

Maxwell

(Age 27)

I get where Ace was going in wanting to take things slow and be friends, yet I couldn't help but feel bizarre about it all. Instinctively, I was an untamed animal. I was lustful and would take every opportunity to bend Ace over and fuck the living shit out of him if given it. Yet, I knew that this was what he needed in order for us to eventually get to that phase. *Go slow in order to move fast*, I kept telling myself.

Venturing out to public places with Ace gave me an unsettling, sinking feeling in the pit of my stomach. What if other people caught on and presumed I was going on a date with Ace Bettencourt? It would be a huge public scandal and I couldn't afford for Brexley Global to suffer because of it. What if the Board retracted their decision in making me CEO of the company? What if they instead made Jasper the man in charge? Then, the corporation would go to shit. That was absolutely out of the fucking question. I couldn't allow it to happen.

I was at a major standstill here. A dilemma. Yet, I knew this was the only way forward. The only way I could get closer to Ace. I'd already experienced what it felt like to have thought that he may never be in my life. It was sickening, and I never wanted to go through those feelings of turmoil ever again. So, there really was no other option for me. I just hoped that the risk was completely worth the reward. And I had a fucking hunch that it truly was.

Luckily, Ace was beyond empathetic and could easily detect the worry I had about being seen in public with him. He booked us a somewhat private dining space at Frevo. As my driver approached the elegant restaurant that doubled as an art gallery, my head darted in every which direction on the streets to verify that no one with cameras was in the vicinity or had followed me here. It seemed as if the coast was clear. Nothing seemed out of the ordinary. So, I quickly opened the car door and made a dash for the entrance to the art gallery. A hostess in all black opened one of the Picasso looking canvases that was disguised as a door to enter the restaurant. "Ah. Mr. Brexley. We've been expecting you. If you would just follow me…" She didn't have to tell me twice.

I trailed behind her, spotting a few other guests in attendance as well at the restaurant, all of which were dressed up and seemed prim and proper, no one that looked as though they had the time or the energy to care about who I was and my business. I could already feel the weight on my shoulders start to lighten as we moved further toward the back of the restaurant. Then, once I saw Ace, the remaining weight practically became a feather. He smiled and waved at me jubilantly. His reaction felt like a shot of Fireball had just poured into my heart, giving it an immediate burning sensation.

I scooted around the table to give him a hug. At the same time, I took advantage of my closeness to him. My nose picked up on the scent of his neck. It was the smell of a warm ocean mixed with traces of bergamot and sandalwood. It felt as if I was inhaling a drug. A feeling of ecstasy overcame me every time I smelled his sexy musk.

So. Fucking. Inviting.

I pulled away from Ace and stepped back, eyeing his body up and down like the savage hawk that I was, admiring my prey that I wanted to feast on so fucking badly. He wore pure white sneakers with slim black jeans. His tight white designer t-shirt showed off the curves of his abs and chest. Over it, he had on an unzipped taupe jacket. Ace was so goddamn delectable. It was a nice invigorating change to see him in something that was more so casual and not the usual attire I saw him in that was meant for a formal event or cocktail party of sorts.

"Glad you could make it," he spoke as I took my seat across from him.

"Of course…" was all I was able to reply with. I couldn't help but continue to stare around the place, hoping I didn't recognize anyone, which I didn't, much to my relief.

Ace lightly sneered, catching on to my reaction. "I get you're nervous, but I think we're safe here. You have nothing to worry about."

I felt his silky, smooth palm placed over my hand. My brain was signaling my hand to shutter and pull away, but it seemed that my heart and other senses in my body were taking over, too overjoyed by his touch to want to withdraw from it. So I allowed his hand to linger on top of mine, at least for the time being.

"I'm not worried," I lied. But I offered him a radiant smile with my response, to make it seem all the more believable.

"Good. You shouldn't be. Anyway," he changed the subject. "I appreciate you being able to take this next step with me… in our friendship."

Friendship.

I know Ace meant it to be endearing, but the word was a dagger that pierced straight into me. I didn't want a fucking friendship with him. I wanted something more. So much fucking more. Did I want to be his boyfriend? I didn't think so. Perhaps friends with benefits, but axe the *friend* part of that equation. Whatever I wanted to happen between me and Ace, I expected it to be beyond a mere *friendship*, as he implied.

But again, *baby steps*. I had to continue to remind myself of this. Ride this long rainbow wave for as long as you can. There will be a pot of gold at the end of it. The pot of gold being Ace's smooth tight ass. I wanted to stick my dick in it and leave it there until it fucking stained gold. That's how fucking bad I wanted it. The real King Midas's touch and all.

And so, I would endure this dinner with him. We would have a normal, casual conversation and laugh at a few jokes over a bottle of Bordeaux. I would be lying to myself if I said that I didn't enjoy Ace's company. This was honestly one of the most authentic dinner experiences I've ever had, where I could let my guard down and be my true self. And it was Ace Bettencourt of all people who could bring this out of me. Maybe this friendship thing with him wouldn't be so cumbersome after all.

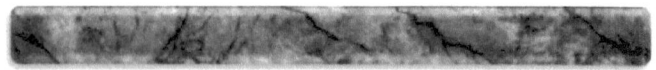

Twelve Hours Later...

Article Post from the Gossip Tea Column

Images surfaced last evening of long-time bachelor and heart-throb Maxwell Brexley holding hands with gay, businessman and socialite, Ace Bettencourt at Frevo. The two were caught in an intimate embrace over red wine and a candlelit dinner. This comes as a surprise to everyone, especially to all the women who have had dreams about landing the sexy tycoon. Sorry ladies! Too bad for them that their potential in snagging this man and living the lifestyle of champagne wishes and caviar dreams just went down the chute.

Even more astonishing, beyond the idea of Maxwell Brexley being openly gay, is the fact that he is possibly dating none other than the protégé of Bettencourt Corporation, long-standing rivals of Brexley Global. Will this modern-day Romeo and Juliet story stand the test of time? Will these two men who should be branded as enemies come out on top together? What will their families think of this shocking revelation? If anyone has the tea to share, it's the Gossip Tea Column. We are on the case.

I woke up the next day to my phone blowing the fuck up. My PR reps were hounding me over this story. Social media and all outlets took it and ran with it. Both my father and mother left me several voicemails. Yet, the one person who I expected to call me and check in didn't bother to reach out at all. Ace had completely ghosted me since this news broke out. It fucking hurt to know that he would leave me hanging like this.

Perhaps I was just overly sensitive at the moment. It was still early in the morning, after all. Maybe he would message me at some point later on in the day. But I was in panic mode right now, circling my high-rise condo with my hands over my face.

What do I do!? What the fuck do I do!?

The cat was out of the bag. The whole world now knew the secret I've kept hidden for all these fucking years. I was gay. And there was no use in trying to deflect from it now. I had so much on the line. My company, my reputation, my pride. I had worked so hard my entire life to build this persona, this reputable and powerful businessman that I was. Now, all of the foundation I had developed could easily crumble beneath me, all because of this stupid fucking gossip.

I should have never agreed to that dinner. I should have never let Ace hold my hand for as long as he did at Frevo. My fist pounded into the onyx countertop of my kitchen island as I passed it.

Fuck it all to hell!

How could I be so goddamn careless!? Well, I actually knew the answer to this already, now that I thought about it. It was Ace. He suppressed the alarm I held. He assured me that I had nothing to worry about. And I fucking believed him.

How the fuck could someone have managed to sneak a picture of the two of us? I vividly remembered the other patrons in the restaurant at the time, and none of them were paparazzi. Not a single one of them stood out as if they had a hidden agenda. But they had to have.

And this led me to a bigger mystery. How could someone have known that Ace and I were having dinner together at Frevo? Unless…

No. Impossible. I couldn't believe I was even fucking thinking it.

Was Ace behind all of it? Was he playing me this entire time? Did he set this entire thing up so that I was forced to come out of the closet? Was it payback against Brexley Global and my family?

I couldn't help but reflect on what that arrogant piece of shit father of his said to me the night of the charity gala. "*At the end of the day, never forget who his father is. I know my son inside and out. I know all the chords to pluck on him and I will always be the one who he listens to when all is said and done. My opinion of him matters to Ace more than anything else in this world.*"

This had to have been all Magnus Bettencourt's doing. That fucking son of a bitch! There was no other logical explanation. No one else would be capable of setting this up but him. The vindictive bastard.

Now, I was unsure of my feelings about Ace's involvement in this whole thing. Was he as equally to blame as his father? I wanted to give him the benefit of the doubt and assume his innocence in all this, but part of me couldn't accept it. He definitely had a part in this whole plot. And there was no way I could let him get away with it. He had played me for a fucking fool. I had lowered my barriers so much, only for him to fuck me over in the end.

There was a sudden banging on my door that distracted me from this mediocrity that I was now dealing with. I opened the door, only to see Cecil standing before me with a smug look on his face.

"And what the fuck are you smiling about?" I accused him. "Do you not realize my entire life is on the brink of fucking ruin? Seriously, someone just took a fucking goddamn wrecking ball to everything I have and now here you stand with a fucking smile on your face?"

Cecil nonchalantly shrugged. "No one cares that you're gay, Max. They'll get over it. It's not the end of the world. Get your shit together, man."

I was stunned by his brash words. Only Cecil could get away with talking like that towards me. Well, he and my father, that is.

"I didn't come here to coddle or feel sorry for you," he continued. "I came to give you an update on Magnus Bettencourt and what dirt I found on him."

If there was anything I wanted to hear besides how I would have to navigate this sticky PR nightmare I was now going through, it was this. Revenge was at the forefront of my mind, and any sordid details I could get my hands on about Magnus Bettencourt I would pay millions for. And hopefully Cecil could give me something of use. "So? What did you find out about him?"

He tossed a manila envelope on my counter. "See for yourself."

Without any hesitation, I reached for the envelope and ripped it open, desperate to see its contents. I skimmed through all of the documents, reports, and images Cecil had collected. As I browsed through it all, I stumbled upon test results of sorts that really captured my attention. Scrutinizing the implications of the test, I lowered the paper to stare directly at Cecil.

"This can't be real, can it!?" I asked with astonishment.

"Believe it. It's all real," he answered.

"You mean to tell me…" I paused.

"Yup. Leo is Magnus Bettencourt's biological son," Cecil finished for me.

"So, what the hell does this mean?" I continued to try to put the missing puzzle pieces together in my mind.

"It means that Magnus has been lying for decades," he interjected. "The story of Magnus taking a stray baby off the streets from some drug dealing prostitute… it's all bullshit. Magnus had an affair with a woman while he was with Vira. The woman chose to keep the baby they had together. Magnus paid her a significant amount of hush money to take the baby off her hands and for her to never speak of it again."

"And no one else knows about this!?" I questioned.

"Not to my knowledge," Cecil replied. "The press would have a field day with this one."

That they would. This was exactly the sort of information I had been waiting for. It was my golden ticket that I needed in order to pay for a chance to ride the roller coaster that would soon be Magnus Bettencourt's life.

Yet, as much as I wanted to get this intel and expose Magnus, something didn't feel quite right about the whole thing. Under normal circumstances, I wouldn't think twice and dwell on it. I would have Cecil do his dirty work and annihilate my enemies, crushing their businesses, their livelihood, and all of their hopes and dreams.

But this was far more complex than any of those other situations. There was more skin in this game than I had cared to want. Ace was now involved. This would hurt him to no end. It would tear him apart. Both he and his brother, Leo. This was life-changing news. Their lives would never be the same again. I had to ask myself, would I be able to live with myself, knowing I had put Ace through all the angst and destruction I was planning for his family to have to endure by revealing this betrayal of his father to the public?

I was instantly reminded of the last time I had damaged Ace Bettencourt, back when we were teenagers at Amplestone Academy. I was reckless, cruel, and selfish. I stole his stuffed lion that tied him to his dead mother. I had vandalized it and left it on a flagpole, dangling in the wind. Was I prepared to be this merciless and malicious once more?

My phone suddenly buzzed on the onyx countertop in front of me. The notification read that it was a text from Ace. Finally, he reached out to me.

About damn time!

His message was simple, and with zero context.

> Ace: We need to talk. Can we meet up? Maybe
> at your place?
> Maxwell: Sure. Does 5:00pm work?
> Ace: Yes. I'll see you then.

I dropped my phone back down onto the countertop. Cecil raised his brow with suspicion. "I need a decision, Max. What do you want me to do with this? This is your one chance at bringing down Magnus Bettencourt. You need to take this shot. Yes, there will be collateral damage involved, but it will all be worth it in the end. What do you say?"

A heavy sigh escaped from my throat. Cecil was right. I couldn't pass up this opportunity. Magnus Bettencourt would do the very same thing if he had similar ammunition against me. But making this decision wasn't an easy one. Far from it. I knew I could be potentially causing irreparable damage between Ace and me by doing this, but what other choice did I have?

"*I'm sorry Ace,*" I mumbled to myself, underneath my breath.

"Do what you need to do," I advised Cecil. "Leak it to the press. And whatever you do, make sure it doesn't trace back to me or Brexley Global."

Chapter 20

Ace

(Age 25)

How could I have let this happen?

I thought I had taken all the proper precautions when it came to finding a safe venue for Maxwell and I have to have dinner at. But I was stupid. So fucking stupid. And holding Maxwell's hand the way I did? Absolutely foolish.

Now, Maxwell was forced to have to come out of the closet because of me. That hurt so damn much. I was the reason Maxwell was in this predicament. I ruined any and all opportunities for him to come out of the closet under his own terms. He would no longer have the freedom to navigate his own sexuality. And it was all my fault.

I felt terrible about it all. I had no idea what to say to him in this moment. I honestly thought it was in my best interest to give him some space, let him figure this out on his own, without my input. I had already caused so much trouble for him, I didn't want to risk adding any more.

Now, I was recollecting everything that happened at dinner last night, trying to remember the few people that were at the restaurant, none of which stood out to me as being undercover paparazzi. It was very possible that it could have been a random person that just happened to recognize me and Maxwell and filmed us. But there was a very slim chance that was the case. No. This person was likely staged and knew exactly what they were looking for. They were tipped off at the two of us having dinner together.

I began to try to narrow down the possibilities in my head of who could be behind this. As far as I knew, only Kent Scythe, my confidante and closest friend, knew about my meeting with Maxwell. But there was no way Kent would do something like this. There was no motive for him to do so.

I then began to wonder just how closely my father kept tabs on me. I wouldn't be surprised if he tapped into my phone or hired a private investigator to permanently keep an eye on me. Magnus Bettencourt was capable of such things. I would be an imbecile to think otherwise.

He is the only person with a motive to want to do this to Maxwell. Even if I was involved and would have to be injured in the crossfire of the war, they had with one another, I'm sure my father wouldn't care one bit. He was all about winning the battle and didn't give a damn about the number of casualties lost in the process. That was in his nature. In his blood. The Bettencourt blood. Thankfully, it was a trait I did not inherit.

I was apprehensive when I saw that my father was calling me this morning. I knew he had heard the news about Maxwell and I caught together holding hands. Half the world knew about it by now, of course. The media had taken the news of the scandal and spread it like a wildfire.

The vibrating and sound coming from my phone was enough to make my heart race a thousand beats per minute. But I knew I would have no choice but to answer him. Postponing a conversation with him would only be worse in the end. Better to just rip the Band-Aid off right away and tackle this head on. I reached for my cell phone and swiped it to take the call.

"Hi, father," I spoke solemnly as if nothing was wrong.

"You really fucked up this time, Ace! I can't fucking believe that not only did you have dinner with a Brexley, but you are now fucking one too!?"

"It's not what you think, father." I continued to speak calmly, despite the irate shouting that was coming for his end of the line.

"Well, tell me what I should think then, son!? The whole world is thinking the same damn thing as me. How the hell am I to explain this to our clients? Our staff? Everyone that matters in our lives, for that matter? You've created one giant PR shit storm for me to deal with now!"

His anger was shocking to me. Unless he was a very good actor, he really was distraught over this entire situation. It made me wonder if he truly was the one culpable for leaking our affair to the press.

"It's really not that big of a deal. We're just friends…"

But those weren't the words he was looking for. He interrupted me, preventing me from even finishing my thought. "Friends!? I don't know about you, Ace, but I don't hold my friends' fucking hands like that. I saw the photos. How could you be such a goddamn moron!?"

"I'm sorry. I truly had no idea anyone was watching. I tried to be as furtive as possible."

"Well, you didn't try hard enough. Now, I must be the one pick up the pieces from this fucking mess you've created!" He let out an angry grunt. "You need to lie low for the time being. I don't want you to step foot out of your apartment. Whatever you do, don't contact a single person until this shit blows over! And don't even think about reaching out to that dirty Brexley. I forbid it! If I, so as much, hear you breathed the same air as him, I will cut you out of our family altogether. You can kiss your inheritance goodbye, the charity foundation goodbye, everything! You'll be disowned forever!"

The dial tone then kicked in as my father hung up on me.

I wanted to punch a hole in the wall, throw my phone to the ground, smash some dishware or plates, anything to get this pent-up rage out of me. I couldn't believe my father and his irrational behavior. He was so over the fucking top right now. But I had to quickly remind myself that this is what Magnus Bettencourt does. This is what he has always done throughout my entire life. If I had a nickel for every time my father threatened to get rid of my inheritance or fire me from Bettencourt Corporation, I would be as rich as we were right now.

But I needed someone to talk to, someone who I could trust and who understood what I was currently going through. And despite my better judgment, I knew that *he* was who I needed in this moment. I too, was probably the only person that could help calm him down too. So, I decided to finally text Maxwell.

Ace: We need to talk. Can we meet up? Maybe at your place?

Maxwell: Sure. Does 5:00pm work?

Ace: Yes. I'll see you then.

The only issue with going to Maxwell's place was that cameras and journalists were scattered amok all around the vicinity. All it took was one shot and then it would get blasted all over the internet and news again that I was seen with Max. Only this time, there was more at stake. If my father were to find out about it, that would be the end of me.

Still, I had to take a chance. I couldn't let Maxwell sit in his apartment alone and go through this. He needed someone by his side. Hell, I did too.

Luckily, there was a private parking garage that not even the paparazzi had access to. The slick black car I was in with its tinted windows hiding my identity went right through it. They must have been expecting me, which is why it went pretty smoothly to get right in.

I drew my hoodie tightly over my head, concealing my face as much as possible. Once the car pulled as close enough up to the side entrance, I bolted right out and into the building just as an extra precaution. Even as I strode the lobby and was greeted by one of Maxwell's assistants, I still kept it up. Finally, once we were in the elevator and the door closed, I pulled it down.

"How is he holding up?" I found myself asking her.

"What do you mean? Mr. Brexley has never been down to even have to hold himself up."

I couldn't help but giggle on the inside. Even his staff viewed him as an invulnerable god.

As we entered his luxury apartment, I stepped into the foyer across the marble floor. "Come. He is waiting in his study." His assistant led the way as I followed behind. She threw open the mahogany double doors and moved to the side to allow me to enter. Then, I saw Maxwell sprawled out across the sofa, with a full glass of whiskey in one hand. The other was held over his face, not even aware that I was in the room.

So much for not having to hold himself up.

I supposed his assistant lied because if word got back to Maxwell that she spoke anything that could be misconstrued as ill-willing, then she would be canned. She knew how to play the game, and I couldn't blame her for lying to me.

Stepping forward, I grabbed a spare glass tumbler on the side table by the sofa he was lying on. The sound of the ice bucket lid popping up, startled him. As I poured myself a drink, he lifted his hand from his face, shocked that I was by his side. I plopped myself down on the couch beside him. He adjusted his legs and feet to give me some space.

"I thought you hated whiskey," he mumbled.

"How would you know that? I don't think I've ever mentioned that to you." I raised my brow, suspicious of how he came to this accurate conclusion.

"That lunch date with you and your father... I could tell you were only drinking it to try and fit in," he further elaborated.

"Really? Am I that easy to read?" I didn't know whether to be ashamed by it or not.

"No. Far from it, actually," Maxwell admitted. "You do make a barely noticeable squeamish face after each sip you take. I'm just observant as hell."

I let out a deep belly laugh, although this was probably not the best of times to be making any jokes. Maybe it was just my nerves, and this was the only way I knew how to react in crisis mode. My version of a psychological defense mechanism.

"So, you don't have to drink it, just to impress me," he added.

But I didn't want to give in. Even now, I didn't want him to always be right. That was the magic of our relationship. We challenged each other and kept it entertaining. So, I brought the glass to my lips and drank half of the whiskey, making sure to show no signs that I was bothered by the potent, strong after taste.

"Stubborn as fuck, til the end," he remarked, with a chuckle behind his voice.

A snicker! At least I managed to get that out of him.
"As always," I replied.

We both sat still for a few seconds, letting the silence linger between us. Neither one of us was fully equipped to have this dreadful conversation with each other about what went down last night and this morning. We were purposefully stalling, trying to avoid the inevitable for as long as we could.

Finally, I gave in and decided to get to it. "I'm sorry, Maxwell. I'm so sorry for all that happened. I was reckless. It was bad enough I thought we would be able to go to dinner together unnoticed. But to add to the poor decision-making, I put my hand over yours in a public place. What the hell was I even thinking?" I thought out loud.

Maxwell then sat up from his reclined position, glancing at me out of the corner of his eyes as he took a drink from his glass. "It's not your fault, Ace. I'm not going to lie. Earlier today, I did question as to whether you set me up or not. But I finally thought rationally and knew you didn't possess a malicious bone in your body. Your father, on the other hand... the verdict is still out on him."

As much as I wanted to negate the idea of my father being involved, I couldn't do it. Me defending my father or saying anything positive about him would only piss off Maxwell and make this entire situation worse. I knew my audience and what he needed to hear in this moment. Max needed my support and nothing else. That's the only thing I would be offering.

"But still, I was involved in it actually happening. We could have easily met privately at one of our apartments for dinner. Now, your secret is out to the rest of the world. And you didn't even get the *choice* to pick a time when you were ready to share that secret." I could feel my eyes watering. A single tear then emerged, running down my cheek. "I forced you to have to come out of the closet, Max. I don't think I can ever forgive myself for this." Then the floodgates opened and out poured the waterfall. I covered my face with my hands, trying to hide my tears from him, but it was too late. I was fully exposed, raw. And he was bearing witness to all of it.

The doors to the study were then shut. I could hear them closing through the sound of my weeping. His assistant must have left to give us some privacy.

I felt a pressure applied to my shoulder. I peered out through my hands to see that Maxwell had his arm wrapped around me, his hand cupping my far shoulder. "It's okay, Ace. Really, it's not as bad as you think it is. I'm actually sort of relieved it happened this way. Otherwise, I'm not sure if I would have ever come out. Now, I can just view this as another business obstacle, something I know I can easily resolve and navigate through. Yeah, it might cost me a few clients and I might have people show me animosity, but it's not the end of the world. It's nothing I can't handle."

He was so strong-willed and so damn sweet to me right now. Why was he the one consoling me, when it should have been the other way around? This was another side to Maxwell I had managed to unlock. A side I never imagined he possessed, yet I was so glad it existed within him. So fucking glad.

"Still, I can't help but feel guilty about all of it. That won't change," I confessed.

"That's okay. You'll get over it. But know that I hold no blame over you. As a matter of fact…" he then paused, scratching the back of his neck like it was a nervous twitch of some sort. "I would do it again, for you Ace. Fuck! I'm not even sure what I'm saying right now."

Maxwell laughed almost deliriously before he continued. "Look. I'm not one who can express their feelings so easily. But there's something about you that I can't wrap my finger around. I keep finding myself drawn to you the more and more I see you. From day one, I knew you were mine, although I may have gone about telling you that in a pretty fucking sordid and vile way, but it's true. I want you, Ace. I want you so fucking bad, it hurts. I hope you've noticed that I'm changing, all because of you."

That's all I needed to hear. Maxwell had shaken me to my core. There were no more games I wanted to play. No more holding back and having him grovel and work to gain my affection. He had done enough. I was ready to put an end to this apology tour of his once and for all.

And to reward him for doing all of this for me, I tilted my neck and leaned into him. It was so sudden. I didn't even have time to process what I was doing. Didn't even give it one thought. My emotions were surging and taking full control. I closed my eyes and pressed my lips against his, tasting the mint and brown liquor from his breath. It was so damn appealing. So damn hot.

I was becoming more abrasive than I normally would, but it felt right. Everything about this felt right. I climbed on top of Maxwell. My legs spread apart, straddling his thighs as I continued to passionately kiss him.

He reciprocated, his hands wrapping around to caress my upper back and neck, pulling me into him. We were desperate to get as close to one another as humanly possible. Deep enough so that our tongues could collide and explore each other's mouths as far as they could navigate.

Was this really happening!? Was this really fucking happening!?

Our past sexual flings were so skewed. It was either him or me controlling most of the situation. But in this instance, we were equals. Both of us were being vulnerable with one another, letting each other take the reins, willing to let the chips fall as they may.

This was exactly what I wanted. What I *needed*. Yes, I was so submissive and weak for Maxwell. But now, I felt confident in myself. I felt strong and still able to give myself fully to him. This was the passion I never knew existed that was now a full force between us.

I was the one who surprisingly took the initiative to remove my shirt, as if my life depended on it. It required me to separate my lips from his for only two seconds, but it felt like a whole eternity. Now that my chest and torso were exposed and his for the taking, I returned to leaning back into him, returning my lips to grace his.

Maxwell's hands trekked down my spine and to the curves of my lower back. I let out a whimper, feeling his manly hands reach lower to cusp the top of my ass. My tight jeans inhibited him from gaining further access.

Even he was annoyed that I was not completely available to him right then and there. He stood up, hoisting me in the air as we continued to kiss, his hands clutching my ass to keep me propped up. He spun around and softly laid me on the sofa on my back, while he stood, ripping his shirt off and quickly pulling down his pants to reveal his rock-hard cock. It was just as magnificent as I remembered it from a few weeks ago.

God, what I would fucking do for that dick!

My submissive personality was starting to come forth, now seeing this godly man stand tall, hovering above me. All I could do was stare up at him in wonder. His hands came forward, tugging on my own pants to pull them off.

We were both fully nude. Our raw bodies were on display for one another. There was nothing else to hide, to snag off. We were officially in the flesh with one another, and it felt like a poetic Michelangelo painting.

I closed my eyes as Maxwell pressed into me. His muscular pecs and arms covered me as he passionately kissed me. I could feel his stiff cock rub against my stomach. The friction against it was enough to cause my own dick to throb. My ass, too, was contracting, begging for his rod to be rammed into me.

"Do you want it, Ace?" he softly moaned into my ear.

God, he was fucking toying with me!

Both of us knew it, but I had to give in. Who wouldn't? Maxwell was an irresistible man. He reeked of sex and masculinity. Everything about him now made me feel possessive all of a sudden. I wanted all of him. I *needed* all of him. His body belonged to me and I wanted to feel all of him in me. I wouldn't be satisfied until I felt him deep inside me, penetrating me, and breeding me so that the intense psychological thrill of a bond was formed.

Maxwell, too, knew it was now or never. The moment we had been waiting for. The moment we had been putting off for over ten years now. It was long overdue. He reached into the side table drawer to pull out a bottle of lube.

I couldn't help but come out of character and raise my brow at him.

Why the hell would he have a bottle of lube in the drawer next to the sofa in his study?

My bewildered reaction was enough to get him to chuckle. "Even in my worst of states, I am always prepared. I overthink and over analyze *everything*. What do you fucking expect?"

For some reason, I couldn't help but picture Maxwell sitting on this sofa ten minutes before I arrived, going through every possible outcome in his head.

He probably thought to himself, *"When he arrives…"*

A.   *Ace will cry with me and we will console each other all night.*

B.   *He will laugh in my face and boast about how he fucked me over and explain how I was a weak bitch for falling for him and his father's plot.*

C.   *Ace will somehow blame fault in himself. I will be the one to console him and we will have the hottest, most passionate and thrilling sex of our lives.*

D.   He will be so turned off by my anxiety and vulnerability that he will be polite and try to leave my apartment at the most appropriate moment.

There were probably other E through J multiple choice options that he had in his own head, but the answer was C. The answer is always fucking C.

When in doubt, always choose C!

My attention rose back to him as he held the bottle of sticky liquid content out, pouring it onto his hand. His fingertips were drenched with the lube. His index and middle finger slowly pressed into my hole as he returned his lips to meet mine. It was so fucking tight.

"Holy shit!" he yelped. "You're so fucking warm, babe."

His literal *warm* words were enough to get me to loosen up even more, to relax and let him gain further access into me. I was convulsing with his fingers buried deep inside me.

"Please," I begged. "Give it to me, Maxwell. I need you inside me."

I wasn't sure what came over me. But I couldn't help but be honest with him. It's what I craved and hopefully he would fulfill this desire I had.

"Oh, you'll fucking get it," he roughly stated. "You're going to get all of it."

Without a moment's notice, he pulled his fingers out of me and quickly used them to slither up his shaft with the lube, before pressing his tip against my hole.

"You want it, babe?" he asked, tempting me.

"Yes!" I screamed. "I need it! Fuck me, Maxwell!"

That's all it took. He immediately plunged into me. My eyes rolled into the back of my head. I was no longer seeing him. I saw nothing but black. The black of the night sky with emerging stars in its sky. They began to shine brightly. And as I came to, I saw those same stars shining within Maxwell's own eyes as he continued to penetrate me.

"Fuck, Ace!" was all he uttered. Sweat was dripping down his forehead as he continued to plow into me. Every thrust that he gave made me want to combust, but I refrained from doing so. I wanted to savor this moment as long as possible.

I could feel Maxwell's cock pulsate even more as it buried itself deep inside me. I could sense he too wanted to cum, but it would be too soon. We had to slow our rhythm if we wanted to extend this moment of ecstasy. And so, we did. After a while, he pulled his dick out of me and flipped me over onto my stomach.

I was on all fours, my butt pressed into the air for him to see. "That ass is out of this fucking world! I've been imagining this for far too fucking long!" he revealed.

The second I felt his cock plunge into me, my eyes bulged. His hand reached around to grip my throat as he continued to pound my hole. Each heave into me became more and more rough.

"Oh My God, Max!" I moaned, in between gasps. "Fuck me, baby. Fuck me like you own me, baby. You do fucking own me. I'm all yours!" I shouted.

"Fuckkkkkk!!!" he screamed in a deep grunt, like a growling behemoth.

And I felt him shaking, panting, gasping. His warm cum seeped into me and I could feel every trace of it linger inside. It was the first time I'd ever had a man release himself into me, and something about it felt so natural and yet possessive. It felt as if Maxwell had now owned me by pouring himself into me, and I couldn't help but be so damn turned on by it.

Max soon retracted himself from me and laid on the sofa. He positioned himself so that I was lying on the inside while he spooned me from behind. His lips nibbled on my neck.

"The things you do to me…" he mumbled.

I grinned at his remark before I glanced up at the clock on the wall. "It's only six o'clock," I informed him. "I could go all night," I further teased.

He shot right up out of his reclined position. "Oh, really!? Is that a challenge, Bettencourt?"

I smiled at how animated he now was. "It's whatever you make of it," I answered.

"Well, how about this then?" he replied. "Let me open one of my best bottles of red wine. We can talk, drink a little bit, and then when I feel in the mood, I'll wrap you up in my arms and fuck you again?"

Damn, Maxwell was already starting to understand how I operated, which I, too, was beginning to learn about myself. "I'd want nothing more than that."

I spun around to face and kiss him some more. Could this get any fucking better?

Chapter 21

Maxwell

(Age 27)

For the first time in years, I slept in the following morning, without waking up to an alarm. Normally, I was strictly regimented with the time I woke up, at 5:30am. I typically started the day off with an intense workout with my personal trainer, followed by a high-protein breakfast. Then I'd proceed to shave, take a shower, and get dressed for work. I was out the door by 7:30am and in the office by 8:00am like clockwork.

But not this time. It was now 8:45am and I was lying in bed holding Ace in my arms, *naked*. I nuzzled my nose and mouth into the back of his neck, getting an extra waft of that spice of his. A hint of vanilla, sage, and something citrusy passed through me. I lightly simpered with delight, enjoying that fucking scent of his.

I never wanted to get out of bed. If I could permanently freeze time and live in this moment forever, I think I would do it. Ace wore me the hell out last night, and based on how late he was sleeping in too, I'm sure I drained the fuck out of him as well. We fucked for what seemed like endless hours into the night, both of us going through two bottles of wine, and we even started on a third before we decided to call it quits.

There was a moment in the middle of the night where I stayed inside Ace for nearly an hour straight. He was ready to lift up, off of me so that my cock would flail out of him, but I held him down. I never wanted to leave from being inside him. So, I firmly gripped tight on him, refusing to release myself from him. He couldn't help but laugh and allowed me to get my way.

Being reminded of that sexy ass of his was what was keeping my morning wood active. But I knew it would be selfish of me to lube myself up and pop it right back into him while he was sound asleep. Although I was now tempted as fuck to feel it again, I refrained from doing so, and continued to spoon him from behind.

Ace squirmed in his sleep and flipped his body over so that he was now facing me. His eyes still remained closed as he breathed heavily in his slumber.

My hands made their way to his head, swiping the little bit of strands of hair he had that were out of place. Now he looked perfect.

Absolutely fucking perfect.

I had no idea how I could possibly be this fixated on another human being. I never saw it coming, yet here it was, hitting me in full force, like a heavyweight boxing glove striking me dead center in the face.

Like a creeper, I just kept my eyes on him, admiring every little detail about him. The gorgeous sway of his hair against the pillow, the perfect curl his eyebrows made, along with his perfectly centered button nose. And those fucking lips of his drove me mad. The plumpness and scarlet hue they held made me wild. I imagined them slurping up and down the long shaft of my cock like they were last night. Another lustful thought that sent a jolt to my dick.

But did I deserve this perfect man? I wanted to believe I did and vice versa with him. Yet I couldn't help but think otherwise. A sense of guilt suddenly washed over me. I was reminded of the decision I made yesterday, a decision that would hurt Ace and his entire family. If I really deserved Ace, I wouldn't be putting him through what I was about to. I wouldn't be the cause of so much anguish and family turmoil he would be experiencing in the near future.

Yet, my tracks would be completely covered. Ace would never suspect that it was me who exposed the licentious details of his father's past. Even if I could potentially come out of this clean, I knew I would feel completely dirty on the inside. In the past, I wouldn't have even given it a second thought. But now that my feelings were growing more and more for Ace, these new and emerging sentiments were hard to shrug off.

What the fuck did I get myself into?

I rolled over to the side and rose from the bed, stealthily enough to not wake Ace up. Reaching for my phone from the nightstand, I decided I would just leave him a lengthy text message as a note, letting him know he was free to stay in my apartment as long as he wanted, but that I would be away handling some business affairs.

As I hit *send*, I moved into my bathroom and turned on the tepid sink water. Cupping my hands, I collected the water and splashed it up against my face. The warm rush instantly woke me completely up. I now just stared at myself in the mirror as the sink water ran. I was looking at the reflection of a terrible person, of someone who was about to start a new relationship off on a lie. I was a deceitful fucking demon, even giving Judas a run for his money.

No. That's who I used to be. That wasn't who I was becoming. *What the fuck was I doing?* I asked myself. Why was I going to go through with fucking over Ace and his entire family? And all for what? Just to get back at his son of a bitch father who was nearly knocking on death's door in the near future? The more I thought about it, the more I realized just how ridiculous this whole thing was. No more. Enough with the pissing matches between the Brexleys and the Bettencourts. It was time to put that all to an end, especially if I wanted Ace to be a part of my life, and I sure as hell fucking did.

I immediately dialed Cecil's number. On the second ring, he picked up. "Yeah?"

"You didn't already leak Magnus Bettencourt's infidelity to the media yet, did you?" I asked.

"No. Not yet. I'm planning on meeting the highest bidder today with the evidence," he revealed.

Phew! Thank fucking God!

"Good. I need you to pull the story, Cecil."

"What? Pull it?" he repeated. "Pull it, as in *withdraw* from sharing it?"

"Yes," I affirmed.

"But why? What gives?" I could practically hear the wheels in his head spinning over the phone.

"I need to put this whole thing to bed. I can't keep going back and forth with Magnus like this. No more slinging our cocks at each other like swords," I explained.

Then Cecil went silent. At least I thought he did, but I could barely hear the faintness of a chuckle in the background, which I suspected was coming from him.

"Are you laughing about something?" I nearly accused him.

"He really has you hooked, doesn't he?"

"Who?" But I knew damn well *who* he was referring to.

"You know who," Cecil replied. "The highest card in the deck," he replied as a code I instantly picked up on.

"Maybe…" was all I uttered. It was the closest thing to an admission I would give him.

"Just be careful, Max. Make sure he is completely worth it to you. If he is, then you know you're making the right choice."

And deep down, I knew that this was the right call. Ace was so worth it, more than I could ever imagine. He had completely changed me. Completely bewitched the living fuck out of me. People always assumed I had an ace up my sleeve when it came to most things, but now I had an Ace that was slowly slithering its way up my arm, past my shoulder and towards my heart.

Chapter 22

Ace

(Age 25)

Without a doubt, last night was the best sex I've had in my entire life. It had been a long time coming. I'd only ever dreamed and imagined that I would finally be fully consumed by Maxwell Brexley. And finally, I had him all to myself. His cock fully immersed in me was the purest ecstasy I'd ever experienced. If I could have sex with him every day for the rest of my life, I would make a habit of it.

I rolled over in his king-sized bed, opening my eyes, realizing it was now morning. I was hoping Maxwell was beside me so that I could propose another fuck session to pick up from where we left off last night. I wanted to ride him so damn bad, but unfortunately it wasn't in the cards. He was nowhere to be found.

I sat up in Max's bed and scanned the room, surprised to see that he was nowhere to be found, much to my chagrin.

Where the hell did he go off to this early?

But how quickly I forgot he was the CEO of a Forbes Top 100 company. Of course, he was already up and likely out of his apartment. Brexley Global couldn't run on its own. I grabbed my phone on the table beside the bed and saw that it was just past 10:00am.

Holy shit!

I assumed it was like 7:00 or 8:00am. I didn't realize it was already this late in the morning. No wonder Maxwell was already up and had started his day. As I checked my phone, I saw a few notifications, including a text message from him.

> Maxwell: Good morning, babe. I didn't want to wake and disturb you. I know how hard you worked last night and figured you needed all the energy you could regain after that exhaustion ;) Anyway, feel free to make yourself at home this morning. Ask one of my assistants if you need anything. Breakfast, clothes, you name it. I'm probably already at the office by the time you read this. Just hit me up when you aren't busy. Looking forward to seeing you soon.

I grinned from ear to ear after reading what could arguably be the nicest message Maxwell Brexley had ever sent to anyone in his entire life. I took a screenshot of it just to hold on to as evidence, to be funny. Who knows? There could come a time when I would need to show him this as proof of how nice and sweet he could be sometimes. Plus, I had an ulterior motive to hold this over Maxwell's head. I knew he would be embarrassed and hate the idea of him being described as kind and sensitive. This would be the perfect way to make him squirm and get embarrassed. I couldn't help but lightly snicker over the thought.

But I was quickly brought back down to reality from this cloud I was resting on. I realized my current situation. It had been a while since I showed my face in public and to my father. If I stayed here in Maxwell's penthouse any longer, he would likely become suspicious as to my whereabouts and could potentially have me sought out. Then, he would learn that I was spending all this time with Maxwell, and that meant I could kiss running the Positive ViBes Foundation goodbye. I couldn't allow that to happen by any means.

I wondered if my mother was watching over me in this moment. What would she think of me being intimate with a Brexley? To be honest, I didn't think she would mind as long as I was happy. That was the kind of person she was, which made me ask the age-old question that I've been asking my whole life. How could someone as compassionate and kind-hearted as her fall in love with my father, who was… a monster?

I would never know nor understand her reasoning, but it wasn't something for me to dwell on. All I could do was remember the fondest memories I had of her and how well she treated me and Leo as we grew up. That's really all that mattered at the end of the day.

Bending over to the floor, I collected all of my clothes and made quick work of getting dressed, before going into Maxwell's bathroom to look in the mirror and brush my hair, trying my best to get myself presentable and together, before I would leave.

Although I had to completely change my mindset and go into business and work mode, I couldn't help but be jubilant and daydream over when the next time I would get the chance to see Maxwell, and what that would entail. I couldn't even imagine how anything that we did from here on out could top last night, yet somehow, I knew it would only get better. At least, that's what I was hoping for.

Before I rolled into my office at Bettencourt Corporation, I stopped by my apartment to shower and dress formally in a suit and tie. Yes, I didn't get in until noon, but hopefully, no one was paying attention.

"Ace, your father is on line one," my secretary informed me. I didn't even have time to sit at my desk.

So much for no one paying attention to my tardiness.

"Yes, father?" I said the second I picked up the phone.

"I need you to come up to my office immediately," he demanded.

"Yes sir. I will be up in a minute," I replied.

Less than a second later, the line went dead, indicating that he had already hung up. Worry instantly overcame me.

He knew I was with Maxwell all night. He had to fucking know. That's why he was so cold and blunt towards me just now, right? Well, not necessarily. He could still be pissed from the previous night. Yes. That's what it likely was. He was just grumpy from still having to deal with PR in handling the news of Maxwell and me being intimate with each other at dinner the other night. That's exactly what it was.

Why was I fretting? I shouldn't be. I was cautious and extremely careful over how I made my way over to Maxwell's last night. No one saw. There was no possible way anyone could have known about my whereabouts. I made sure of that this time around. I had learned my lesson the hard way and I wouldn't be repeating that same mistake ever again.

Striding down the hall and up the escalators, I made my way to my father's office with a confidence in my step, to make sure Magnus was unable to detect any sign of weakness or vulnerability within me. The man was a trained bloodhound for that kind of thing. He could snuff out the deficiencies and frailties in anyone and take advantage of the situation to expose and ruin them for it. Intimidating as hell he was, even to me, his own son.

"Have a seat, Ace," he requested, the second I stepped foot in his palatial office.

I sat in the leather chair across from his desk.

"Is this a matter of urgency?" I asked. "I'm extremely busy with working on planning an upcoming event for Positive ViBes," I further added, wanting to make it seem like I didn't just arrive to work a moment ago and that I was super busy with no time to ever have possibly been able to visit anyone in the past twenty-four hours and have the greatest fuck of my life last night.

"Are you really that busy working on that?" my father contradicted. "Because you could have fooled me. I heard you were busy at Maxwell Brexley's home last night. Actually, I was told you spent the night and didn't even leave until 10:30am this morning. So, you tell me Ace, what were you really fucking working on? Because right now, the only thing you're really working on is my last fucking nerve!" His tone instantly changed, and I knew I was going to get the worst reprimand I would ever get in my life.

I was in disbelief. He must have had someone follow me. It was absolutely ridiculous.

Insane!

Yet, I knew it wasn't in my best interest to call him out on how much of a privacy violation that was, to have me followed everywhere I went. Instead, I took the apologetic route, as I often did with him.

"I'm sorry, father. I couldn't help it. I just needed to…"

But his loud voice overrode my soft one. "Who do you think you are, Ace!? Do you think you can just deliberately disobey me and get away with it? Do you think it's fucking funny to nearly ruin this company and all that I worked for, all over some gay fling!?"

I shook my head. "No, of course not."

"Well, tell me what to think then, Ace? What the hell has gotten into you? You're not thinking clearly and I need someone who is able to, who actually wants to be CEO of this company. Meanwhile, here you are fucking around with a Brexley like some high school girl."

His words were so cruel, so fucking derogatory, but I couldn't speak up.

"I don't think you're in the right head space to even run Positive ViBes…" he continued.

"No!" I nearly yelled. "I am more than capable of managing the charity foundation. I've worked so hard on it. Don't let this one bad decision take away from all that I've done for Positive ViBes."

"I'm sorry, son. You leave me no choice. I warned you what would happen if you contacted Maxwell Brexley, yet you went ahead and did it, anyway. Surely, you were prepared for the consequences of your actions. Risk versus reward…"

But before I could even chime in and counter his argument, his office doors banged open with a thud. The noise made my neck spin around quickly, nearly giving me whiplash.

And there he stood. Maxwell had his arms folded over his chest, just glaring at us from across the room in his pure black suit, like the cool, calculated and powerful onyx demon that he was. But what the hell was he doing here? What was the meaning of this?

Chapter 23

Maxwell

(Age 27)

Something didn't settle well in my gut with all of this. I had every opportunity to wreck Magnus Bettencourt. Bettencourt Corporation would be demolished if I let Cecil leak the story to the press. But I couldn't hurt Ace. That's who was most important to me in all this. Even if he suffered just a little bit from what would go down once Magnus' past infidelity was revealed, I still couldn't allow him to go through that miniscule amount of pain.

I needed to protect him. And there was no way I could go through with being the root cause of what could tear him and his family apart.

Damn myself for being so weak!

Why was I letting my heart lead the way for once in my life!? I swore to myself I would never allow such a fucking thing to happen, yet here I was, choosing to let it guide my decisions over my brain. I knew it was the better business move for Brexley Global to spread the news that Magnus Bettencourt was a filthy, disgusting pig. A month ago, I would have completely exposed him for the despicable fucking leach that he was. But now, that was no longer the case.

Even as I told Cecil to call off the entire plan of fucking Magnus over, it felt like karma didn't do its full job. Out of all of us, Magnus was the one walking away from this whole ordeal as clean as a whistle. He was the one who tried to screw me over countless times. It was he who was nothing but a terrible father to both Ace and Leo. So why should he be able to get out of this situation without learning his lesson? That I couldn't allow to happen. I needed to be both the judge and the jury in making him suffer. His verdict was clear as day and it was about time I was the one to deliver it.

I barged right into his office unannounced. Luckily, Ace was already there, so I didn't have to bother to somehow get him to arrive here so I could divulge all of Magnus's vile secrets while he was present.

"Ah! Magnus, thank you for inviting me over here on such short notice," I greeted him with.

The old bag rose from his seat. His eyes were widened, likely stunned by my presence. "Oh? Maxwell. Glad you could come. It's ironic that you showed up at just the right time. I was just telling my son of what a foolish mistake he is making by coercing with you. Clearly, Brexley Global is on the brink of ruin because of everything that you two have done. Yet, Ace chooses to make his bed with you and so he must lie in it."

Yeah. He'll lay in my bed every night and morning for the rest of his life. Fucking stupid old man. I want to Ace to do just that. He should be running into my arms. The further away from you, the better.

"On the brink of ruin?" I repeated. "Far from it. If anything, our clients have showed nothing but support for my coming out. Furthermore, we've gained more investors as a result of this news. You have done me a damn solid favor, good old man."

I could see Magnus's lips curl into a deep grimace. He was not pleased with this information one bit. "Bullshit. I know there are plenty of clients of yours who have yet to reach out to you. They'll pull out of their contracts with Brexley Global in the near future. There is no doubt about it."

I nodded. "Perhaps we will have a few who decide to terminate their agreement with us. And that's their prerogative to do so. But I wouldn't be so worried about my investors, Magnus. If I were you, I'd be concerned about your own."

"My investors!? Just what the hell do they have to do with any of this?" he asked.

"Well, if they were to ever find out about the secrets and scandals that *you* have kept from them and the rest of the world, and your family, for that matter, surely they will go running."

"Again, you're full of it," Magnus deflected. "Your back is against the wall and now you're just trying to come at me with a blank gun. No ammo. A desperate attempt if I ever saw one."

"That's where you're wrong," I began to explain. "If anyone's back is against the wall, it's yours. Tell him," I demanded, pointing at Ace. "Tell your son the truth about what you did all those years ago. What the real truth is about Leo and his mother. Go on."

Magnus stood up and laughed in my face, still playing dumb as fuck. "What the hell are you even talking about!?"

"The story you made up about finding a stray drug dealer off the streets and taking Leo in. All of it is a complete lie. You made the entire thing up. You cheated on your wife with a random woman. That woman became pregnant with your child." I proceeded to step forward and tossed the manila envelope Cecil gave me onto Magnus' desk. "All the evidence is there. The blood tests, the proof of payment that you gave Leo's mother as hush money. All of it. Are you still going to sit here and deny it!?"

Ace's mouth gaped. He stared at Magnus with bewilderment. "Father, tell me it's not true. It can't be…"

Magnus grabbed the manila envelope and began tearing it apart into shreds.

"You fool," I remarked. "I have copies of all the content within that envelope. You're not getting rid of it that easily."

Magnus then stopped. I could see that his face was turning beet red. He was frustrated as hell that I now was the one holding the cards. All the cards, including the very ace that he claimed that *"at the end of the day, he'll never forget who his father is. I know my son inside and out. I know all the chords to pluck on him and I will always be the one who he listens to when all is said and done. My opinion of him matters to Ace more than anything else in this world."*

Now the tables were turned. I was the one with the ace in my hand. He had neglected it for far too long. Now, he would live to regret it.

"Father…" Ace said once more.

"Fine!" Magnus gave in. "Yes. I did it. But it was almost thirty years ago now. Even if you go to the media with this, they won't give a shit."

"But that's where you're wrong," I began to elaborate. "They'd have a field day with this. You being unfaithful to your wife? The fact that you claimed to have an adopted child for nearly thirty years only to know all along that he was truly your biological son? Do you honestly think everyone is going to be okay with this fucking terrible course of action?"

Magnus raised his hands in the air as if in defeat. "Tell me," he stated. "What's your price? What do I need to do to keep you from revealing this to the press?"

Oh Magnus! You fucking simpleton!

I would have accepted millions of dollars and stolen major clients of his and would have brought them over to Brexley Global in the past. But now, I had much greater goals and plans for the future that I would easily give up those millions of dollars for.

"I don't have I price," I replied. "I don't want your money, Magnus. I'm not going to tell anyone else outside of this room about what I know about you being Leo's true biological father and all. And you can thank your son for that." I nodded in Ace's direction as I said this.

A huge weight had been lifted off of my shoulders and it felt damn fucking good. This was the right thing to do. The rush of goodness that surged through me made me realize this.

I turned my back to Magnus and Ace, proceeding to head out of the office. As I reached the doors, I tilted my head around to face the both of them. "And I fucking love your son," I confessed. "I love him more than you ever fucking possibly could."

Chapter 24

Ace

(Age 25)

I couldn't believe this! Did my father just admit that he cheated on my mother and had a love child with another woman!? Did he confess to lying about Leo being his adopted son for almost three decades? This was all too much to process. Leo really was a Bettencourt. He was my half-brother all along. How could my father do something so evil? So monstrous?

"Ace… I…" Magnus began to say.

But I couldn't let him finish. I had heard enough. My father was always quick to interrupt me whenever he deemed necessary. Now it was my turn to cut him off.

"No. I've heard enough out of you, father. I cannot believe what you did. To Leo, to me, and most importantly to my mother."

"I'm sorry, son. It was thirty years ago…"

"What does that have to do with anything!?" My voice rose. "If it wasn't for Maxwell, I'm sure you would have taken this secret to the grave."

"I would have come out with it, eventually," he tried to explain.

"No. I don't believe you would. You're that fucking selfish of a human being. And you have the audacity to sit here and tell me how I'm the one that has made all the wrong decisions that could ruin our family name and business? You were so quick and willing to just dispose of me and remove me from the company altogether, while you knew in the back of your mind that you were holding on to a deeper and darker secret this entire time."

"Ace, I know I haven't been the ideal father, but…"

"I'm done! There is nothing more you can say. I really don't want to hear anything else come out of your mouth. I'm the one calling the shots now. And you will listen to me or else I will take you down so damn hard that everything you worked for will get destroyed. Bettencourt Corporation will tank if you don't do as I say," I threatened him.

"And what will you have me do? Go to the press and tell them all that happened? That's out of the question," he stated.

"No. I don't want that information out there in the public. And not for your sake. For mine and Leo's. Here's what's going to happen. You will resign as CEO of Bettencourt Corporation, effective immediately. We'll put out a statement letting everyone know of an early retirement you're planning."

"And then what? Who is going to run Bettencourt Corporation? Do you think I'm going to just hand it all over to you?" he asked.

"No. I will still oversee our charity foundations. You will make Leo CEO. He is the next in line and deserves the title more than anyone. It's what he's been working towards all this time. He's earned it, especially after what you've put him through now all this time," I elaborated.

"You really want this to happen?" he checked with me.

"Yes. And if you don't do your part to make it work, I will leak your infidelity to everyone. Your reputation and name will be ruined. You will have no legacy."

Magnus let out a deep sigh. For the first time in forever, he was finally defeated, by his son, no less. "Very well. But the second you and him fuck things up for the company, don't come crawling back to me to try and fix things for you. Because once I'm out, I'm out for good."

"No problem there. We'll handle everything on our own without you," I replied.

I stood up out of the chair and walked towards the door. This meeting was over and I had nothing more to say to him. Oh… except one thing.

"And there's something else you need to do," I stated.

"Which is?"

"You will be the one to tell Leo the truth about who he really is. And about his mother. You'll do it sooner rather than later."

"Fine," he gave in. "I'll do it soon."

"Oh. And father? I hope we can all recover from this."

For some reason, Magnus was now laughing. "We are a pretty fucked up family, aren't we?"

I nodded. "And all of this time I thought it was the Brexleys who were the ones that were fucked up."

I ran out of Bettencourt Corporation as fast as I could, hoping to catch up with Maxwell. I sprinted out of the main lobby doors and out onto the streets, scanning up and down the road, looking for any sign of him. Just in the nick of time, I caught the tail end of him getting into the back of his private car.

"Maxwell!" I shouted, just before his door shut.

I ran over towards him, trying to get past all the pedestrians that were in my way. Luckily, the car remained still and his door then re-opened. His leg stepped out of the car, much to my relief. He stood up and glanced around every which direction, wondering who was shouting his name.

Once Maxwell saw me approaching him, he couldn't help but grin. "Ace. What are you doing out here? Shouldn't you be with…"

"My father?" I interjected. "I already handled things. He will be stepping down as CEO. Leo will run the company from now on."

"And what about you?" He raised his brow at me.

"What about me? I'll continue overseeing Bettencourt's charity foundations. Philanthropic work is my calling. It's what I love. I wouldn't want to give that up for anything else."

"As long as you're happy, then I don't care what you do," he replied.

I smiled at him, showing off my bright pearl ivories. As we stood just inches apart, I turned to the side to see that we now had an audience. People had their phones pulled out, videoing us. Not to mention a few cameramen managed to make their way over to the area already.

"Maybe we should…" But before I could even finish that sentence, Maxwell was already leaning forward. His lips pressed against mine to shut me up. I closed my eyes and fell victim to his passion, wrapping my arms around him.

I tuned out the shouts and some gasps that people gave to us, continuing to kiss Maxwell wildly. After a few seconds, he withdrew his mouth to catch his breath, pulling away from me. I still had my hands over his shoulders and behind his neck. "Are you sure you're okay with this?" I asked worriedly, wondering how he was handling all of the cameras and phones that were recording us, that would likely post this video and images of us to social media and blogs, further confirming our intimacy with one another.

"Let them all watch," he announced. "I want the world to know I'm gay and dating Ace Bettencourt, the hottest guy out there."

I held my hand over my mouth, trying not to laugh. Secretly, I was glad he was able to be this open about us now. I, too, wanted everyone to know that I was with America's top bachelor. Both girls and guys would be completely jealous that the sexy, debonair Maxwell Brexley was now off the market.

"Well, as long as you're comfortable with it, then so am I," I replied back to him.

"Then it looks like we're on the same page," Max added, as he opened the back car door open, ushering for me to get in. I obliged and hopped in as he sat next to me and closed the door.

"Where are we going?" I inquired.

"My place," he quickly answered.

"Oh. Why are we going there?"

"Because I need you in my bedroom so I can rock your fucking world."

And I wouldn't have it any other way.

One Year Later...

Chapter 25

Maxwell

(Age 28)

My whole world had changed now that Ace Bettencourt was in my life. I felt freer in some way, even though I was technically tied down now with a boyfriend. Now that the public knew I was gay, I no longer lived in fear or in hiding, worried that someone would somehow find out about my secret and expose me, ruining my life and all that I had worked for.

It made me feel so much lighter, and less fucking grumpier for sure. But I couldn't just contribute my change of heart to that. Ace, too, was majorly responsible for my more optimistic personality. He brought out the best in me. Hell, we both actually brought out the best in each other.

Leo Bettencourt smoothly transitioned into the role of CEO at Bettencourt Corporation. I was actually his mentor over the past year, helping him along the way. He wouldn't dare ask Magnus for any assistance. It had now been months since their father actually communicated with them. I knew he would come around eventually, and I was prepared for that time to come. Who knows, I may even be invited over to the family dinners if the Bettencourts ever had them again in the future.

Speaking of family dinners, Ace was already welcomed into my family with open arms. My mom was more thrilled than anyone when I had informed her I was *settling down* with him. Jasper and Charlotte were also supportive of the entire thing. It was my father that took the most time to come around. But as time fast forwarded, and I brought Ace around my family more often, my father eventually learned to accept that I loved him, even with him being a Bettencourt and all.

I stood out on the balcony with a cup of coffee in hand, in nothing but my black boxer briefs. I stared out into the pure white sands that led to the cerulean blue ocean. Ace and I had booked a week-long trip to the Maldives together, except we now had an entire private island all to ourselves. The Coco Prive Kuda Hithi Island Resort was just ours for the entire week. Not that we even needed six villas, a whole wine cellar, and three pools, one of them being a forty-meter infinity pool all to ourselves. However, we made it fun and decided to stay in each of the different villas every single night we stayed down here. Needless to say, we had sex in every single one of them, claiming our territory in each.

I wanted this vacation to last forever but knew that was an impossibility. I had a whole corporation to run, while Ace had plenty of charity organizations to keep afloat. So, we would just enjoy the time off we had together, even if for only a week, and make the most of it, which we were already doing, just soaking in each other's company, making the best fucking memories with one another.

My ears perked up at the sound of loud water pressure coming from inside the villa. Ace must have been taking a shower. I couldn't help but display a diabolical grin on my face. He should know better than to be taking a shower without me in there with him. I dropped my coffee mug on the railing and strode inside towards the bathroom to see that Ace was already soaking wet under the water. His hands covered his face as he pushed his hair back.

God, he was so fucking sexy!

I couldn't get enough of him.

Furtively, I stripped off my black boxer-briefs and entered the shower behind him, while he was facing the opposite direction with his eyes still closed. Once I had him right where I wanted him, I pressed my hand against his throat, pinning him to the wall.

Ace jumped at first, completely startled by the reaction. My hand lightly squeezed his neck as we stared into each other's eyes, the water pelting us in the face. He grinned as he studied me, while I, too, smiled, almost demon-like.

I lightened my grip on him so he could speak. "Déjà vu," he commented. "I'm starting to think that this is what has turned you on all along."

"Something like that," I remarked, before tilting my chin to lean forward and kiss him, almost maniacally, while my hand still rested on his throat.

"You always like being the predator, don't you?" he asked me.

I nodded. "Of course. Especially when you are such an enticing, submissive prey."

A few months later…

Chapter 26

Ace

(Age 27)

The Annual Brexencourt Charity Event was underway. Victoria Brexley and I decided on a new name for the gala since it was now a yearly joint collaboration between the two of us. We liked the sound of Brexencourt, even though Maxwell gave us both a hard time about the name, saying he didn't want the world to pick up on it and start referring to me and him as such.

"I don't want people turning us into a *Bennifer*, *Brangelina*, or some dumb shit like that." He spoke on it with such seriousness. But Victoria and I assuaged him, saying it would never come to that. Unfortunately for us, we couldn't control the media, nor did we have a magic mirror ball to predict that that was what would actually happen. When Page Six and other gossip columns got photos of Maxwell and me, they started shipping us as the *Brexencourts*. Eventually, Maxwell became a good sport about it, having to just get used to the name. There was no way of changing it. He knew it was better for him to just roll with the punches.

In the event hall, I sat at a circular table with Leo, Jasper, Kent, and Cecil. Maxwell was on an important business trip that he could not back out of, so he was missing the event this year. He sincerely apologized about the scheduling conflict, but I assured him that it was okay. I even got on my knees after the conversation just to show him *how okay* I really was about it.

The six of us became a tight pact in the last year, practically doing everything together, from attending major parties and events with each other, to vacationing together, and even hosting more private poker tournaments at one another's homes. Soon, it became apparent what we all were and why the six of us clicked so easily. In the past year, Leo and Jasper also came out as gay now that Maxwell had paved the way for them.

The five of us were all now out of the closet together, except for Cecil, who kept his cards held tightly close to him. Who knows who or what he was into? He was so damn mysterious, but all of us knew better than to question him. That is everyone except for Kent, who got a rise out of riling Cecil up all the time.

The blogs and gossip pages dubbed all of us as the *Bosses of Bane*, the city's most successful and sexy CEOs with an edge to them. Now that was a name that Maxwell could easily get behind. Needless to say, he loved the sound of it.

I was carrying on in conversation with Leo, Jasper, Kent, and Cecil at the table when someone came up from behind me, placing their hands softly on my shoulders. I glanced over to see that it was Victoria Brexley.

"I don't mean to interrupt, but could I have a word with you, Ace?" she requested.

I nodded. "Of course." I rose from my seat, and we began to traipse the dining hall, her arms wrapped in mine. "What is it you wanted to talk about, Victoria?"

"Well, Paige Lacardo is here tonight. She is running a full cover story on our charity gala. She wants to interview you if you'd be up for it."

"Oh! Well, yes, I would love nothing more than to gain more exposure for us. Where is she now?" I inquired.

Victoria pointed in the direction of the balcony. Curtains covered the French doors leading out onto it. The area was off limits to our guests. It was a liability concern if anything. An open bar plus a balcony with a ledge equals a recipe for a disaster.

"She's outside, waiting for you," Victoria explained.

"Alright. Let me just grab a glass of champagne and I'll head on over to her."

Victoria released her arm from mine and headed off in a different direction of the party. I moved towards the closest waiter, who held a tray with full champagne flutes. Grabbing a glass, I took a few sips before making my way towards the French doors. I couldn't help but reminisce about the time I followed Maxwell out here nearly two years ago. It was when everything changed. That was the night we started our entire relationship over from scratch. Everything that happened after that night would just get better for us, from then on out.

As I approached the doors to the balcony, I pushed the curtains aside and reached for the handle, opening it. As I stepped out into the brisk cool air of the night, I was rendered still and speechless. Before me were hundreds of lit candles of different sizes and shapes. Rose petals were spread all across the entire surface. A red carpet led out from the spot I was standing at right to the end of the balcony. And at its end was where he stood. The Onyx Demon himself, dressed in his traditional all black suit. I held my hand over my mouth in disbelief.

What the hell was this!? What was he thinking?

The entire scene felt like I was on the finale of the Bachelor. The views were more decadent than anything I'd ever experienced in my entire life. There was only one direction for me to go. So, I slowly paced down the red carpet, spinning around to get a full glimpse of every intricate and gorgeous detail that was laid out before me. Then, I finally reached Maxwell at the end of it all.

He grabbed my hands and held them in his. I knew exactly what was coming, which was why the waterworks started their flooding right away.

"Here," he said with a chuckle, handing me the pure black handkerchief from his suit.

God, even his handkerchief was pitch black, just like the onyx he adored. But honestly, I would have it no other way. It was what drew me into him from the beginning. I loved Maxwell for who he was, and I wouldn't change a thing about him.

"Thank you," I softly stated, wiping the corners of my eyes with it. We then laughed together, nervously.

"I'm sorry I lied about the urgent business trip, but it was the only way that I could surprise you and plan all of this," he informed me. "Ace... you have to know how much I fucking adore you. How much I fucking love you. When we were teenagers, I was a complete and utter asshole. A hot-shot who thought he had the world wrapped around his fingers. But then I met you. There was something about you that intrigued me and that I even felt threatened by. So, I hurt you, in the worst possible way. Once we parted ways after Amplestone Academy, I thought about you a lot and that kiss we had together. I thought the only way I could have you was by *owning* you, treating you like one of my staff members. I know it was awful to think that way."

I couldn't help but smile, being reminded of how ridiculous and crazy our journey was together over the years.

He then continued. "But you stood your ground. You gave me a wake-up call and a dose of my own medicine, which was exactly what I fucking needed. You made me realize how much I wanted you and how I would need to change in order to have you in my life. You opened up so many new doors for me. New beliefs. A whole new outlook on life. You've changed me so much, Ace. Without you, I would still be that awful person that I was years ago. Now, I'm so blessed to have you in my life. And I want nothing more than to make you the happiest man on Earth."

It was then he kneeled down on one knee, reaching into the pocket within his jet-black blazer, pulling out a small box. He opened it, revealing to me a gorgeous diamond wedding band. The lights from the metropolis above us reflected off of it, making the ring shine brightly.

"Ace Bettencourt, will you marry me? Will you deal with me and my fucking shenanigans for the rest of our lives?"

I busted out in laughter at that last part, but nodded without any hesitation. "Yes! Of course, I will, just as long as you can accept us being known as the Brexencourts," I replied.

I held my left hand out for him to place the engagement band around my ring finger.

"Oh, the sacrifices I have to make," he sarcastically said. "It'll be a hell of an inconvenience, but what the fuck. I'll have to deal with it." We continued to laugh with one another.

I was shocked to see a single tear creep out of the corner of his eye. I'd never seen Maxwell cry, ever. This was completely new to me. I had to call him out on it.

"Is that a tear I see?" I asked, trying to rile him up.

He shook his head. "Just allergies…" he deflected with.

I grimaced. "Sure. We can just go with that."

I didn't even realize that a full party had collected on the balcony. Maxwell's family and our friends all surrounded us. They sprinted forward to peck their kisses on our cheeks, give us hugs and handshakes full of congratulations and showed us nothing but love.

"I can't believe you said yes," Kent joking whispered in my ear. "That's an intense lifelong commitment there, buddy. Don't forget it."

Jasper then came close to me. "You and my cousin are really going through with this, eh? He's a pretty fucking lucky guy."

"Yeah. I love him, Jasper. And I couldn't picture my life without him. We complete each other."

He couldn't help but smirk at me. "I figured as much. I just can't believe the effect you have on him. It's damn crazy."

Other friends and family then shoved their ways in to make their sentiments and feelings known about how pleased they were with the engagement.

Maxwell and I entertained them all for nearly another hour or so, before they all parted ways and returned inside per the instruction of Victoria Brexley. The charity gala was still occurring after all, and so dinner would proceed on schedule as it was meant to.

Now it was Max and I that stood alone on the balcony again.

"So why did you pick here of all places to propose?" I asked him now that we had the privacy. I had a hunch as to why but wanted the confirmation.

"This was where it all started," he began to explain. "This was where you allowed me to absolve myself of all that I put you through in the past. It was here where you said the slate was clean and we could begin getting to know each other without our past encounters coming back to haunt us. I thought it fitting that this be the very place where I propose to you, and we continue our journey together."

So. Fucking. Poetic.

Maxwell continued to surprise me more and more with each passing day. "I think that's so damn beautiful," I revealed to him.

"Not as beautiful as you, Ace. On both the inside and out," he replied, before leaning in to passionately kiss me

"So, where do we go from here?" I asked him.

"Who the fuck cares? As long as it's with you, I could care less where we end up," he stated.

"Well, you are my Onyx Demon," I commented. "Would you care if we ended up in hell together?" I inquired jokingly.

"Not one bit. I wouldn't mind testing it out and seeing if hell is really hotter than the sex we have together," Maxwell said.

I take it back.

I smiled, thinking to myself.

There were some things that I didn't change about Maxwell Brexley, and nor would I want to, because that was what I fell in love with about him to begin with, flaws and all.

Acknowledgements

Thank you, Matt and Ed, for being my rocks during this writing experience. You've helped me so much along the way.

Have to give a big shout out to my friend Cate and my amazing Instagram family and friends. Your support and affirmations mean the world to me!

Thank you to my Spectrum Books family. It was a pleasure to work with each and every single one of you. I look forward to working with you all on future projects as well.

And thank you to my mother Gina, brother Jimmy, and the rest of my family and friends for your love and support.

Most importantly, thank you to the LGBTQIA+ community. I will continue to support my community and give us more fun reads in the near future!

About the Author

B.J. Irons works in the field of education as a college professor and educational leader. Many of his personal experiences as a gay man have contributed to his books. Being a part of the LGBTQIA+ community himself, B.J. hopes to continue to bring more colorful and fun fictional works to his LGBTQIA+ readers.

Other Titles by B.J. Irons

The Greek Mythologay Series
Meduso: Book 1
Arrogance: Book 2
Orpheus: Book 3
Hermes: Book 4
Hephaestus: Book 5
(Coming soon)

The Bosses of Bane Series
The Onyx Demon: Book 1
The Jasper Devil: Book 2
(Coming Soon)

Stand-Alones
The Cul-de-Sac
Rippling Waters
Sinfluenced
The Gift That Keeps on Taking
The Fire Island Ice Queen
Second-Guess
Master of the Bluffs

Excellent LGBTQ+ fiction by unique, wonderful authors.
Thrillers
Mystery
Romance
Young Adult
& More

Join our mailing list here for news, offers and free books!

Visit our website for more Spectrum Books
www.spectrum-books.com

Or find us on Instagram
@spectrumbookpublisher